finding grace

Alyssa Brugman

Published by
Delacorte Press
an imprint of
Random House Children's Books
a division of Random House, Inc.
New York

Visit us on the Web! www.randomhouse.com/teens
Educators and librarians, for a variety of teaching tools, visit us at
www.randomhouse.com/teachers

Library of Congress Cataloging-in-Publication Data

Brugman, Alyssa.
Finding Grace / Alyssa Brugman.
p. cm.
Summary: Undecided about her future after graduating from high school,
an Australian girl takes a job caring for a brain-damaged woman.
ISBN 0-385-73116-7 (trade)—ISBN 0-385-90142-9 (GLB)
[1. Brain damage—Fiction. 2. Caregivers—Fiction. 3. Australia—
Fiction.] I. Title.

PZ7.B82835Fi 2004
[Fic]—dc22
2003062563

The text of this book is set in 11.5-point Janson Text.

Book design by Angela Carlino

Printed in the United States of America

November 2004

10 9 8 7 6 5 4 3 2

BVG

acknowledgments

Many thanks to my mother, Lynette, who never wishes me luck but instead encourages me to do my best. Thanks also to Nicole, Robyn, Dirk, Peter and Therese, who told me that they liked it, which gave me the confidence to find out whether maybe someone else might too.

finding
grace

Grace had a brain injury. That's just how she was.

She spent a lot of time sitting in her leather wing-backed chair just staring out the window. I didn't know what was happening inside her head, and I didn't really think about it.

I was eighteen and knew everything. Well, not *everything*, but I did know a great deal about a great many things. For example, I knew that time healed most wounds and those that it didn't you simply got used to.

That was before I met Grace or Mr. Alistair Preston.

I was sitting on the stage at my high school graduation. The principal was standing at the lectern pontificating to my hungover, tired and emotional classmates and their thank-God-the-Higher-School-Certificate-is-over parents. Most of the girls were weepy. There had been some strenuous merrymaking going on the night before.

I was looking out at my fellow students and casting my verdict about their collective destinies (because I was eighteen and knew everything, well, not *everything*, but I did know, for example, that birds have to flock together, whatever their feather, in the schoolyard. It's just one big aviary and if you're a little sparrow you'd better make yourself as inconspicuous as possible).

I was glad to be leaving school. Our school was just about the most concrete place you can imagine. The playground was concrete. The canteen area was concrete. The bus stop was concrete.

What was the Department of Education thinking? "Hey! Look at this design, it's simplistic, it's raw, it's low-maintenance. It says 'place of learning.' Let's build it!" Or maybe there was another, more sinister purpose in mind? Maybe this concrete school was an experiment in elementary forces as a form of discipline?

Anyway, in my tired and emotional state, I was looking out at all my ex-classmates and thinking that I'm the worst off of the lot. At least they didn't have the superbright lights shining in their eyes. How much more conspicuous can you be?

I looked over at Mr. Preston sitting next to me. He's the "distinguished, pillar-of-the-community" guest. He's one of those really rich fellows giving back to the community.

He had a notepad on his lap, and was stroking his chins, listening with interest to the principal's speech, jotting down notes. He looked down ("studying," *snort*), so I leaned over and had a really good look. He was chunky with broad shoulders and a bit of a belly—"a veranda over his toy shop," is what Nanna would have called it. Nanna came from the mobile-home side of the family and had a whole swag of analogies for human reproductive organs that she had no qualms about including in any conversation.

Mr. Preston had a commanding presence. He looked to me like a no-nonsense chap. I could imagine him as a secret agent with a tuxedo on under his wetsuit. It was a stretch, but I could imagine it.

I looked down at his notes.

Ladies and gentlemen, firstly I would like to thank you for the opportunity to speak here today, blah, blah . . .

Curriculum. Aware of the dedication and commitment required, blah, blah . . .

Be bold, don't settle for mediocrity, have fun . . .

I couldn't believe my eyes! The man was writing his speech! Right there on the stage, seconds before he was supposed to say it! More, he had seriously written "blah, blah . . ." as if he was going to make those bits up as they came to him. Up here! In front of five hundred people!

I'm having a quiet panic for him. I'm thinking that he's never going to make it. I'm getting embarrassed for him already. I'm squirming in my chair, I'm going red.

That's one of my problems. I turn red at the drop of a hat. I have see-through skin. I am so white, I'm the whitest person you can imagine. My skin is my greatest enemy. It betrays every emotion that I have. I'm happy, I blush. I'm sad, I blush. I blush, I blush more.

The stupid thing is, I don't even have to be having an emotion. I don't have to be embarrassed or angry or anything. I can just blush totally out of the blue. It's as if I've been going through "the change" my whole life.

I've developed a number of defensive responses to it, though. For example, if I can feel a blush coming on, in my head I'm saying, "Oh, my God, I'm going to blush. No, Rachel, don't do it, don't do it, here it comes," and then I just turn around and run away. It doesn't matter if I'm in the middle of a sentence, I just run out of the room. Then, when the glow has subsided, I stroll back in as if nothing has happened.

Or the other thing I do (and you may consider this to be a bit childish), if I feel a blush coming on, is to start looking around at anything other than the person I'm talking to. I look over their shoulder or pretend to be really interested in something behind me. My rationale is that they will be so busy trying to figure out what I'm looking at that they'll ignore the fact that the person they're talking to has just been magically replaced by a gigantic tomato. Or maybe I think that if I'm not looking at them, then they're not looking at me.

I told you it was childish.

As a result, I think I have a reputation for being quirky. Quirky is neither conspicuous nor attractive. Have you ever heard a boy say, "I really like that girl, she is so quirky"?

Anyway, I'm sitting onstage wriggling and glowing a lovely fuchsia—nowhere to run. I examine my fingernails and let my hair hang down over my face. Mr. Preston turns toward me. He has a serious frown happening, or that might have been his normal expression. Old people tend to have their most common expression permanently entrenched in wrinkles. Anyway, he has this stern gaze happening and he says, "Ants in your pants?"

I haven't heard that expression since I was five years old. No-nonsense chap indeed!

I whisper, "Is that your speech?" He's nodding and clapping for the principal.

I've spent more time studying the speech I'm about to make than my three-unit English text. I'm about to tell him this when the principal introduces him and he stands up. He smiles at me, while I'm having mild apoplexy on his behalf, and says, "Easy-peasy."

I'm sorry, was that *easy-peasy*? Two infantile expressions in a row. Pop goes the commanding presence.

"Ladies and gentlemen, firstly, I would like to thank you for the opportunity to speak here today. I feel very honored." He puts his hand over his heart.

"Secondly, as a contributor to your school, I am aware of the dedication and commitment required in undertaking your studies. My heartfelt congratulations to each of you," he says, looking out at the faces in the crowd. "What an amazing achievement." He stands back from the microphone and claps. "Please, ladies and gentlemen, put your hands together for these incredible young people."

"OK"—he pauses and rubs his jaw—"I've prepared a speech here about citizenship and how it was in my day." He waves the notepad in the air above his head. "But I think you've had just about enough lectures." He turns, puts the notes down, winks at me, turns back and grips the sides of the lectern.

"Please, allow me to offer you three pieces of advice before this boring old man sits down and lets you get on with your celebrating.

"One"—he pauses—"be bold. Never miss an opportunity to let your brilliance shine and dazzle. Take a chance. Accept the challenge, or if the challenge doesn't arise, make your own challenges."

He frowns and looks earnest. "Two, don't settle for mediocrity. Find a dream and pursue it. Let every decision you make bring you closer to achieving that dream.

"And three"—he smiles and nods—"have fun. Take time to play, because if you're not having a good tear-squirting belly laugh, chances are you're not doing it right.

"I will not wish you good luck." He stops and looks out at the people. "I don't believe luck to be a necessary ingredient for success. Instead, I wish you the wisdom to make good decisions. Thank you for your attention."

He stands back from the lectern and nods while the people clap. He waves at the crowd as he is walking away from the microphone, like the President of the United States or Nelson Mandela or something. The audience is still clapping. Everyone's emotional. That's what happens when you've had no sleep and your life is all over the shop. Everyone's entitled to get a little teary under those circumstances.

Mr. Preston shakes his head, smiling. They're still clapping after he's sat down.

●　●　●

Afterward I'm serving tea and those little triangle sandwiches that always have stringy limp lettuce and some kind of canned fish on them, doing my last prefect duty. Mr. Preston is poking them down his neck, whole.

"You're Rachel," he says, consulting his program. "What are you going to do when you grow up, then?"

I'm so sick of this question. When you're doing your HSC, everyone asks, "What are you going to do?", "What are you going to do?" After a while it is difficult to withhold the urge to scream, "I DON'T KNOW, MAN! I'm just trying to finish what I'm doing now!"

I really don't know what it is that I want to do with my life. Maybe science? I'm good at science. I'm good at English too. How do you really know what you want? Even if you do know what you want, how can you be sure you'll end up there anyway? I look at the shop attendants behind the counter and wonder. I sit staring at the back of the bus driver's head and think, "Is this what you always dreamed of? Or do you just *do*? How did you end up here, anyway?"

Instead of screaming at Mr. Preston, I say, "I've applied for a science degree. I'm interested in pursuing marine biology, astronomy or forensic psychology, but I haven't decided on a specific field at this point."

My mother insists that "I haven't decided on a specific field at this point" is a more civilized response than "I don't know, man." I think she's probably right.

The speech is over, the paracetamol is kicking in, I've finished school forever, and I'm feeling a little brazen.

"So," I ask, "what are *you* going to do when you grow up, then?"

He places the teacup gently in the saucer and smiles at me. "I'm going to drive a fire engine."

•　•　•

The second time I met Mr. Preston, I was at work. Working is much easier than school, because someone approaches you once a week with money. That never happens at school, unless you are a drug dealer.

My job was to make cappuccinos and toasted sandwiches at this funky café down at the end of the main street. It's an old warehouse done up in stainless steel.

There are tables out on the footpath looking over the harbor. As the sun sets, the smog from the industrial sites wafts out over the water, turning the horizon a magnificent tangerine. At night the industrial lighting from the shipyards dances out across the water on little rainbows of spilt oil and diesel and the tankers float silently past.

The staff in the funky café wear those long black aprons that are "en vogue." All the waitresses except me have short hair in vibrant colors. I can't wear my hair in vibrant colors. It clashes with my blushes. My hair is long and straight and a blondey brown. Very boring, but at least it blends nicely with my blushes. If one is going to have a neurotic episode that manifests itself in a physical form, it's always nice to be matching.

I'm serving those little triangle toasted sandwiches again. Light meals seem to be my lot in life. It doesn't pay very well, but dollars are dollars and it's nearly Christmas. My mother always makes a big deal about Christmas.

My mother makes a big deal out of every possible celebration. Sometimes I will come home and find her in a cardboard sombrero and there will be my brother sitting at the table in a newspaper poncho and all of a sudden it's Mexican night at our place. We have impromptu theme nights all the time. My mother loves to celebrate. She's having a good life.

My brother's name is Brody. Apparently, my mother was all set to call him Benjamin but when she was in hospital, somewhat altered by painkillers, flipping around the Bs in the baby-name book, she came across *Brody—an unusual beard*. She laughed and laughed.

I thought it was funny too, until I looked up my name. It means "ewe." My mother always looks at us with this little twinkle in her eye. We are an endless source of amusement to her.

Anyway, Mr. Preston wanders in and orders a short black to go. He looks at me, frowns and looks away. He's leaning his arm on the counter. He's dressed in a really expensive-looking plum-colored suit. I'm pouring coffee into the little Styrofoam cup.

Everyone in the café is digging Grace Jones' "Walking in the Rain." That's how funky this café is, they play late-seventies music with pride, and the punters love it.

Mr. Preston turns toward me again. I can tell he's trying to place me. I put the coffee on the counter and say, "Easy-peasy." He smiles. "That's right," he says, "and you're the astronomical forensic biologist."

He pays and saunters out of the café.

• • •

My third encounter with Mr. Preston was at the café again. It was lunchtime and we had the whole back section booked for a suit function. I was in the kitchen, stuffing vol-au-vent cases. The chef was having an anxiety attack. The chef always had an anxiety attack when there were more than three tables occupied at any one time.

The chef was sautéing fillets of veal and weeping and singing "Somewhere Over the Rainbow." Every now and then he would turn to me and shriek, "Oh! It's all too much, Toto."

Mr. Preston left an envelope on the counter. Inside was a short note and a newspaper clipping.

You seem to be a bit of a bright spark. While the world of marine psychology eagerly awaits your contribution, perhaps you may wish to consider this challenge?

POSITION VACANT

Live-in carer required to assist female with personal and domestic duties. Furnished accommodation provided close to shops and university. Experience in the area of disability care desirable but not essential. Suits student/nurse/OT or similar. $'s negotiable.

2

i took the ad home to my mother. She frowned.

I've started to consult my mother about things that happen in my life. A couple of years ago I would just wait until she was concentrating on something else, like watching the news or reading, and I'd tiptoe into the room and say in a quiet voice something like "I'm going to buy a pony, if you don't say anything in the next three seconds that means I'm not allowed . . . (*one*, *two*, *three*), thanks, Mum."

Now I've discovered that she actually knows more than I do. It was a revelation to me, given that I'm eighteen and know everything—well, not *everything*, but certainly an enormous amount about a number of things. For example, I know that no news isn't necessarily good news. It may just mean that the bad news is delivered to you far beyond the time in which steps could have been taken to remedy the disagreeable situation.

The discovery of my mother's wisdom happened one afternoon when I was chatting to her over an ice-cold red cordial. We were sitting out back, on the veranda. There was no particular theme that afternoon (although I'm sure if I had given my mother the opportunity she would have said "Australiana," on account of the furiously blossoming melaleuca).

I was telling her about one of my school friends, Amanda, who was moving in with this absolute Neanderthal. He's an apprentice tiler and the most intelligent conversation I have ever had with him was when he was really stoned (and that *always* makes for sprightly repartee, doesn't it?).

Bozza (as he was known) was providing me with a blow-by-blow description of how he had learned that day that you can't put the cut edge of a tile in the bottom row of a shower because the moisture seeps in and discolors the tile. He was talking in a monotone. I could almost see him sounding out each syllable in his mind, much like a small child trying to build a scale model of the Anzac Bridge with Popsicle sticks and crepe paper.

So, I was telling Mum how I thought I should tell Amanda that it was a mistake.

"Rachel darling," Mum said, "what do you suppose that will achieve?"

"Well, she won't move in with him."

My mother shook her head. She said, "No, she *will* move in with him, and she won't be your friend anymore, and if she did want to move out again, she wouldn't turn to you for help, because it would give you the chance to say 'I told you so.' "

I took a sip of my red cordial, listening to the clinking of the ice cubes, and thought about what she had said. It occurred to me that she had been using that technique on me for years and I hadn't even noticed.

So I showed her the ad and she frowned.

"It says close to shops and uni," I said, nodding and hoping that she would nod too.

"It sounds like a big job, darling."

"Nah," I said, waving my arm in the air, "it's just like babysitting."

She shifted in her chair but said nothing.

"I'll be earning money just by sharing a house. How good is *that*?"

"But it's not just sharing a house. You will be responsible for another person. You'll be *responsible*."

"But I'll be earning money and it's close to uni."

She sat back in her chair and crossed her arms. "Well, you can do whatever you want, but I just want you to think about something; when you're at uni you'll be studying. It's hard work. When you're not studying you're going to want to go out on the town and make new friends or meet boys. You're going to want to bring friends home. You won't be able to do that."

I suddenly felt sad. I don't have many friends. There's Kate that I work with at the café and a few friends from school but they are mostly my friends because we were in the same class. I'm a bit of a loner.

I wanted to tell my mother that I'm not ready to go out

on the town. I don't know about boys and clothes. Other girls at school seemed to know about this sort of thing by instinct. Not me. I'm just a plain old sparrow. This job would suit me because it would give me an excuse. I could tell myself I wasn't going out because I was working, not because no one had asked me.

"It can't hurt to go for an interview," I mumbled.

My mother rubbed my shoulder and smiled. "You do what you want to do, darling. I just want you to be happy."

• • •

The interview was held in an office building in the city. It was a private nursing agency that provided "carers" at an hourly rate for elderly or disabled clients.

I was interviewed by the manager of the agency and (surprise, surprise) Mr. Alistair Preston. The manager was an attractive woman in a conservative navy pinstriped suit. She smiled, shook my hand and thanked me for coming.

I was to live, rent-free, in a two-bedroom house near the university. I was to receive a wage of $135 a week.

$135 a week! Boggle, boggle.

I was to care for a brain-injured woman named Grace. For between fourteen and twenty hours a week I was to be relieved by a nurse, who would administer Grace's physiotherapy.

"Since Grace came out of hospital she has been cared for by this agency," said the manager. "We have provided a series of nurses on a rotational basis twenty-four hours a day. We have been more than pleased to offer this service; however, this kind of care is unusual for us. Grace is an unusual client because there is no primary carer.

"Our normal service is to provide relief to the primary

carer of the client, usually parents, adult children or other family. As part of the service we hold six-monthly evaluation consultations with the client's doctor and family."

Mr. Preston leaned forward. "At the last consultation we discussed the adverse effect of this constant stream of new faces on Grace's progress. We haven't seen any improvement since she's come home. We're not sure that she will *ever* improve, but we have decided to introduce a primary carer. This person, having almost constant interaction with Grace, will be in the best position to note any behavioral changes. The agency will continue to relieve that primary carer, as they would for other clients."

"But I have no training," I interrupted.

"Her condition does not necessarily require formal training," the manager explained. "She can walk. She can feed herself. But she doesn't do anything without direction. She can hear but she doesn't respond and she doesn't speak. You will require some initial training, first aid and so forth. We hold courses here and have taken the liberty of allocating a place for you and the other applicants in the class commencing Saturday. Otherwise, the role is not dissimilar to that of a nanny. Of course, as part of our service, a nurse is available immediately if you need help."

I guessed it was light meals and cleaning for one.

No problem!

3

i received my letter of acceptance into a science degree at Newcastle University on a Thursday. I should have been more excited, but I had worked hard at school so it was no less than I expected. I had reaped what I had sown. I had made hay while the sun shone.

I started my training course for the job on the following Saturday. On the first day I learned how to make a splint, how to deliver CPR and how to help someone who is choking.

I worked in the café with Kate in the afternoons. She's a couple of years older than I am. Kate is one of those slim, funky people who can wear short hair.

I can't wear short hair. I look like a boy—an ugly boy with a bad haircut.

Kate can start fashions. She could wear a sack, and have people say, *"I just love your hessian tunic, where did you get it?"* They would just say to me, *"Excuse me, why are you wearing a sack? Are you protesting about something?"*

I hope one day I can look as relaxed as Kate does. She has been at uni for about six years. Her student loan debt would probably be equivalent to the gross domestic product of a small nation. She's doing engineering and has the most enormous brain, so she'll probably be able to afford it.

While we're cashing up at the end of the day I tell Kate about the new job.

"How 'community sector' of you," replies Kate, smiling.

"What do you mean?"

"Don't get me wrong—that sounds great! It's just that, well, you struck me more as a kind of reclusive private-sector research type, that's all," says Kate. "I always pictured you in some brutally white laboratory sewing body parts on mice, or something."

"Really?"

"Well, yes. You always look so diabolically cerebral," she replies.

I might have to work on my image.

"I thought I looked quirky."

"Oh, of course," says Kate, "but in a kind of clandestine, bizarre way. You strike me as someone who is always amusing herself with some private joke."

I frown, counting the coins as I slide them off the counter and into my palm.

"I'm sorry," she says, "have I burst your self-esteem?"

"Well, yes! I thought I appeared to others as sort of cute

and quirky, like a . . ."—I scratch my forehead trying to think of an appropriate analogy—"like an overbred Weimaraner pup."

"Well, of course you look like an overbred Weimaraner pup," said Kate, "crossed with say . . . Gargamel, or maybe Doctor Elefan?"

"Oh."

• • •

I'm a little perturbed. I think about it on the way home. Firstly, Gargamel and Doctor Elefan are both *boys*. Secondly, they were both ugly—really ugly! I can't believe it! If one is going to be likened to cartoon characters it would be nice if they were roughly the same gender at the very least!

At the end of the first aid course Mr. Alistair Preston phoned me. I told him that I'd been accepted into the university. He congratulated me and then said, "Over the last few months we have interviewed a number of candidates, none of whom have been satisfactory for a number of reasons. I talked to your principal at your graduation. We have been friends for many years. She described you as being responsible, intelligent and having a delightfully quirky sense of humor."

There's that word again.

"Your manager at the café, who is also an old acquaintance of mine, said you were punctual, hardworking and excellent with customers. We have discussed your suitability on the basis of these references and your competence during the course, and have decided that with adequate support from the nursing staff, you should be more than capable. And given the wage and the proximity of Grace's house to the university, you should still be able to pursue your studies."

"Great," I said.

"Do you still want to do it?" he asked.

"Yes," I replied.

"It's not going to be easy," he said. "How about we take you on trial?"

What is this? Nobody thinks I can do it. My mother doesn't think I can do it, Kate doesn't think I can do it—and now even the guy who's offering me the job is questioning my ability.

I got an A+ in snakebites and hyperventilation. What's so hard about it? What do I have to do to prove that I'm capable?

"I'll do it."

i drove my car to my new house on a Saturday and arrived exactly on time.

I have a car that's older than I am. Sometimes I have to pump the brakes before they work. The car goes through more oil than petrol. Also, steam blows in through the heater vents straight from the radiator and it doesn't turn off. It would be less of a problem if the windows opened properly, but they don't. This is not a bad thing in winter, because the hot air from the radiator keeps me warm, but in summer the condensed water and coolant can be pungent.

I've been concerned about the effects on my health of breathing coolant. That can't be good for one, can it? So I keep my trusty snorkel on the passenger seat and when I drive I poke it out the narrow slit between the pane and the seal of the driver's side window.

Anyway, I found the house. The street was probably once a main thoroughfare, but the end has been blocked off with giant plane trees reaching over and meeting in the middle. It's cool and quiet, except for birds.

Three blocks away is the "restaurant strip." There are heaps of restaurants, Mexican, Italian and Turkish. I love Turkish. I love sitting on those little cushions. Then there's the "contemporary Australian cuisine." I wonder if it's known as "CAC" in the biz?

As far as I've observed, contemporary Australian cuisine means that instead of laying the food out flat on an ordinary plate, they pile up the food in a cone shape in the middle of a very big plate.

Anyway, the house is lovely and cozy like the ones you see in those country magazines. There are agapanthus bobbing about in front of a white picket fence and overgrown daisies in pink and white poking through the pickets. Pavers warped by flourishing weeds lead to a small front veranda.

The front door to the house is open. I can see down the hallway straight through to the dappled green and yellow light of the back garden. The hallway has a high ceiling. I can hear the hollow clop of footsteps on a polished timber floor. I can hear the echo of voices from inside the house.

Down the hallway there are two open doors opposite each other. The bedroom on the right is yellow, the same as the hallway, and the other is cream. I can see a large mahogany four-poster bed and cream mosquito netting pulled back with two big satin bows on the wall. I hope that's my room.

Farther down the hallway is an opening to the kitchen.

Soft light comes through a large skylight. There's a bookcase, floor-to-ceiling, on the far wall, filled with cookbooks, ferns and crockery.

As I stand in the doorway to the living room I see two women. One is wearing bright pink rubber gloves. She's sitting on a hearthrug on the floor in front of a big stone fireplace, rolling a glass vase in newspaper with her legs stretched out on either side of a cardboard box.

She picks up the vase and shoves it into the box. The mantel is bare, probably because all the ornaments that were on it are now wrapped in newspaper in the box on the floor.

The other woman is wearing denim overalls and her lips are pursed. She's standing in the middle of the room facing the woman in rubber gloves, with her hands on her hips.

Some people look exactly like an animal, or what an animal would look like if it were turned into a person. The woman in denim overalls with the pursed lips reminded me of an animal.

What does she look like?

Now let me just say up front—I'm as tolerant as the next omniscient eighteen-year-old (who knows everything, well, not *everything*, but I do know, for example, that a watched pot *will* boil eventually), but in the first thirty seconds I didn't like the look of these women. I didn't like their hair. I didn't like their clothes. I didn't like their shoes.

Rubber Gloves looks to me like one of those competitive mothers at school—the ones who do canteen duty not out of the goodness of their hearts but because they are busybodies; the ones who think Presentation Day at school is Best Parent Award Day.

The tall one? I guarantee that her car is just riddled with man-hating bumper stickers, and stickers that start with "Honk if." How can you respect anyone who looks like they have "Honk if" bumper stickers?

"Well, you can't have the piano," announces Rubber Gloves, brushing her gloves together. "I've already booked a piano tutor for Jeremy. I've paid for three months of lessons up front. A kind aunt wouldn't break little Jeremy's heart."

I peek around the doorframe and see an old upright piano on the far side of the fireplace.

The lady with the tight mouth frowns. "Well, you know I'll be taking a few of those vases you've got there *and* the lamp table." She talks very quickly and shakes her head. That's something else for me not to like about her.

"Angelica is having the lamp table. We have already agreed on that," says Rubber Gloves.

Tight Mouth sniffs. "Well, I'll be having the leather armchair then." They both turn away from me. It's then that I see the third woman in the far corner of the room.

She is sitting in a dark mahogany wingback chair with a green throw rug over her legs. Her hair is lank and dirty and hangs in her face. Her mouth hangs open. She is twisted around looking out the window with vacant eyes and absently stroking a small black cat in her lap.

"Jesus, Brioney!" says Rubber Gloves. "She's still *using* the leather chair. What? Are you just going to tip her out on the floor?"

Tight Mouth tosses her head. "We'll get her another chair. She can have the one in the shed."

I drop my suitcase loudly on the floor. Both women, startled, turn back toward me, and then glance quickly at each other.

"You must be the new nurse," says Rubber Gloves. They both beam at me in the most insincere way.

"We were just getting rid of a few of these old things, so there would be more room for you," says Tight Mouth. "We've been just dying to get in here and have a good cleanup. You know, tidy the place up a bit."

It looks to me very much like they were stealing stuff.

"There's no need really, this is all I've brought with me." I point to the suitcase on the floor. "Just my clothes, really."

They glance at each other again. "Well, we'll just get a few things out of your way and then leave you to settle in."

Rubber Gloves struggles with the box of newspaper-wrapped objects. "Well, are you going to help me or not?"

They drag the box toward the door.

"Put the box down," comes a deep, quiet voice from the doorway behind me. Both women flinch, a little squeak escaping from Tight Mouth. I turn around and see a *large and growly bear.*

"Alistair!" They say in unison. "How lovely to see you. We didn't know you were coming today. We were just tidying up a bit."

"I said put the box down."

They both let go of the box and it thuds to the floor.

"Now empty your pockets."

"Come along now, Alistair, surely that's not necessary?" says Tight Mouth. "Is it, darling?" She turns to Rubber Gloves for support.

"I said empty your pockets!"

Rubber Gloves reaches into her pockets and pulls out car keys. "See?" she smiles.

Tight Mouth crosses her arms across her chest.

She squeals as the large and growly bear charges over to her and thrusts his hand into the breast pocket of her overalls. "This is outrageous!"

He holds his fist in front of her face. Entwined in his fingers is a fine gold bracelet with a heart-shaped clasp.

"She doesn't *need* it anymore."

"Get out! Scavengers!" he roars.

Mr. Preston is holding the gold chain up to his face, the fine links resting in the palm of his hand.

I'm still standing there with my suitcase at my feet.

Without even acknowledging me, Mr. Preston walks hastily over to the woman in the chair. He kneels before her, brushing her hair back from her face, hooking it behind her ears. The large and growly bear is gone.

"Hello, Grace." He holds her face in one of his large hands for a moment. Then he loops the gold chain around her wrist and fastens the clasp.

The woman sits looking out the window with the small black cat on her lap. The cat stretches, yawns, its green eyes blinking as it regards Mr. Preston, an intrusion into its sleep.

The woman doesn't stir, she doesn't respond at all.

Her hair is a little bit longer than shoulder length, dark brown and quite thick with little ringlet curls at the ends of it. She has dark shapely eyebrows and big, dull brown eyes. Her dark pink lips are full, but hang loosely.

She looks oddly like Snow White. I'm going to live with Snow White.

Well, I'm certainly not Prince Charming but I could pass as a dwarf, surely?

5

Mr. Preston showed me around the house. "This is your room," he said, standing back so that I could enter. My room was the yellow-painted one. The timber floor continued in here and was covered with a pale blue rug.

A brass double bed with a fancy country quilt in yellow and blue flower prints stood in the center of the room. Next to the door there was a pale wooden dressing table ("distressed," I believe, is the technical term for the effect, although this one looked quite sedate—boom, boom!).

"Grace's room is across the hall." I followed him into the cream room. Beside the four-poster and two bedside tables stood a rocking chair. Soft billowy cream curtains covered French doors that led out to the veranda.

On the right side of the bed was a walk-in wardrobe. "You can walk through here into the study," said Mr. Preston, demonstrating.

I poked my head through the wardrobe into a small room, with books and a computer. That would come in handy.

"Down the hallway, living room to the left, kitchen and bathroom," he said, pointing to the closed door.

Mr. Preston picked up the cat and laid him on his back on the inner curve of his arm. "This is Prickles."

I raised an eyebrow. (I can do that. I inherited it from my mother. It's very useful—particularly when you can't think of anything clever to say.)

"Prickles?"

"It's a long story."

I often amuse myself by thinking of cool names for pets. I think a good name for a small dog would be Eccleston. There's a place on the way to where we used to go camping when I was little. We would drive along and there was a sign that said "Eccleston." Then there was a church and a house and then there was a sign facing the other way that said "Eccleston."

I want to buy a small dog and call it Eccleston because it wouldn't be far from one end to the other. I'd be amused every time I saw him. I'm very much my mother's daughter.

Mr. Preston leaned his forearm against the doorjamb above his head. "What do you think? Are you OK?"

"I'm OK."

"You'll be fine. I'm here most days, anyway, keeping the vultures away." He smiled.

"Are they your sisters?" I asked.

"Heavens no, they're Grace's sisters." He cocked his head and looked at me with a little frown.

Then who is he? I mean, what is he to the Grace woman?

"Are they paying for me?"

Mr. Preston smiled on one side of his mouth. "I don't think so. Essentially Grace is paying for you. I take care of her finances and legal matters."

So, he's her lawyer or accountant or something. Still, he's pretty attentive, considering.

Mr. Preston's mobile phone rang. He lifted it out of his breast pocket. "Preston."

I watched him while he was talking. His phone voice was deeper and booming. He paced about, frowning and running his fingers through his hair. At the end he dropped the phone back into his pocket.

"I have to go. I had intended to stay longer."

Mr. Preston said goodbye to the Grace woman and then left in his big dark car, promising to come back tomorrow.

I stood in the living room with my hands on my hips. The Grace woman was in her chair. I wasn't quite sure what to do.

"Umm, do you want to watch telly?" I said to her.

Silence.

Her head hung to the side a little and she leaned awkwardly, like a rag doll, in her chair. Her eyes were glassy and unfocused. A little drop of spit formed at the side of her mouth and trickled down over her lip, leaving a small dark stain on her shirt.

I looked away quickly and examined the room.

"Umm . . . where is the telly?"

Silence.

I walked over to the cupboard opposite the lounge and opened the doors.

"Here it is." I pointed in the cupboard and looked over at the Grace woman. She stared straight ahead. A thin string of saliva dangled from her chin.

"I guess you knew that already," I mumbled.

Silence.

I bent down to take a closer look at the telly.

"Umm . . . where are the buttons?"

I stood back and turned around in a circle.

I closed my eyes, put my fingers to my temples and tried to turn it on using Vulcan mind power.

Nothing. I'm assuming you need to be a Vulcan.

I heard a thump on the timber floor. Prickles jumped down from the windowsill and sauntered into the kitchen. He sat down next to his bowl. He looked in the bowl, looked at me, looked in the bowl, looked at me, winked at me.

"Don't wink at me, you saucy devil," I said as I walked toward him into the kitchen.

I could feed the cat. That would give me something to do.

"Are you hungry, puss? Do you want to eat something?" I explored the kitchen cupboards. There wasn't much—lots of spices, flour, dried pasta and condiments, but nothing to make a meal with.

I found a box of dry cat food and some tins in the kitchen cupboard and poured some of the dry cat food in the bowl. Prickles sniffed at it. He put his tail straight up in the air, gave it a little shake, sauntered back into the living room and jumped on the couch.

I walked back to the telly cupboard. When I leaned toward it I saw a remote control tucked in the back. I stood back and started pressing buttons.

I picked up the cat and sat with him on my lap.

"Do you want to watch something, puss?"

Flick, flick, flick.

"You know, puss, I don't think there are enough American sitcoms in this time slot."

Flick, flick, flick.

"Huh, would you look at that? Kramer just fell through the door again. Who would've thought he'd do that? Every episode it's a surprise."

Prickles and I watched two hours of sitcoms. I gave him a scintillating commentary.

At nine-thirty I pulled at the Grace woman's shoulders. She stood up, and I walked behind her, pushing her by the small of her back into the bedroom.

Rummaging around in her wardrobe, I found a T-shirt and a pair of boxer shorts. I peeled off her tracksuit, trying to avoid touching the spittle. She sat on the bed in her underwear and looked blankly over my shoulder. Her stomach hung out and her shoulders slumped.

I blushed while I reached behind her and unclasped her bra. I felt her breath on my neck, and smelt it—sour and cloying. I pulled the shirt and shorts on her, tried not to look or think about it too much and dressed her as quickly as possible.

I pushed her into the bed and pulled up the covers around her neck.

"Well, then. Nighty-spritey."

The Grace woman closed her eyes and I sat on the edge of the bed and looked down at her for a little while.

I noticed that her leg was tucked up in an uncomfortable way, so I pulled the covers back and straightened it.

It was weird. I hoped I was doing it right. All I did was move her from one room to another.

I walked through the house, switched off lights and checked that all the doors were locked. I left one of the back windows open so Prickles could hop in and out.

I sat on my new bed, put my hands out behind me and swung my feet back and forth like a little kid. This was my room, my home now, my first home away from my real home, where my mother was.

I knew I could do this. It would be easy. It was going to be just like babysitting except that the Grace woman was quieter and I wouldn't have to play with her.

I'd started a new job. I was a grown-up. Except I didn't feel like a grown-up, I mean, I knew most things—not *every-thing*, but I did know, for example, that if someone were to offer me a gift horse, the first thing I should *not* do would be to look it in the mouth. I would be far more likely to wave my arms about and shout, "What the devil am I to do with this, then?"

My first day alone with the Grace woman was fairly hectic. Actually, it was a disaster. I woke up in a strange bed in a strange house. When I looked at the clock, I could see that I'd slept in, which was unusual because I'm a morning person. Always, since I was little, as soon as I opened my eyes I would jump up! I'd skip around, ready for another exciting day.

I always do a quick lap of the house just to check if anything has changed in the last eight hours. This isn't as silly as it might sound, you know, because in the whole course of my life there have been seventy-two separate occasions when some person or being has entered the house while I have slept and left gifts or chocolates or both. You never know unless you check.

My mother is Dutch, so we celebrate both Christmas and St. Nicholas Day. We also celebrate a variety of other days that may have origins in religion but are much more likely to be inventions of my mother's. Blueberry Day springs to mind. On Blueberry Day we wear blue and celebrate the blueberry by eating blueberries in endless combinations: blueberry pancakes, blueberry pie and, of course, what Blueberry Day would be complete without fish in blueberry sauce?

Of all the fruit-based celebrations that my mother has held (Avocado Weekend, Lime Day, Mango Week), Blueberry Day has been the most consistent. The most memorable, however, would be the Inaugural Lychee Day 1988.

It was remarkable for two reasons, the first being that it was the one and only time I inquired after my father. My mother, in a manner that I can only describe as *wildly* uncharacteristic, blanched and then said very quickly, "It doesn't really matter. Have another lychee." She then proceeded to poke lychees down my neck in an exceptional display of dexterity.

The other reason that Lychee Day was remarkable and, I imagine, the primary reason why it has not been celebrated since, is that it became apparent early in the day that Brody reacted to lychees with explosive diarrhea. (As if normal diarrhea isn't unpleasant enough!)

Later, on Lychee Night, I found my mother crying. When she saw me she wiped her eyes brusquely with the back of her hand and beamed at me. It was the first time it occurred to me that perhaps she wasn't invincible.

Anyway, I have never questioned any of the mythology surrounding any of these customs (nor ever asked again about the other source of my genetic makeup). If these people/creatures wish to leave presents around, fine.

So I jump up. No presents this morning, unfortunately. I make myself some coffee and toast and curl up on the lounge to watch some cartoons. Watching cartoons makes my eyes sore. I think it's because I forget to blink.

After about an hour I walk into the Grace woman's room. She's looking fairly uncomfortable. As I help her up I can see, and smell, that she's wet the bed.

How disgusting! I put my hands up to my face and turn around in a circle, wondering what I should do.

I take her to the bathroom, take her clothes off and put her in the bath. I'm trying not to look at her naked. She lies there in the bath, staring at the ceiling. I quickly look in the bathroom cupboard and find some bubble bath. I whisk at the water between her feet so the bubbles will foam up and cover her body.

Then I strip her bed and put the linen in the washing machine. There's a plastic undersheet on the mattress. I lift that up by the corners with my fingers, trying not to touch it any more than necessary, and take it into the laundry, plunging it into the tub.

Washing has always been my job at home. My mother is a big fan of division of labor. I was responsible for washing everything—floors, dishes, clothes, the car. Brody's job used to be waste disposal but he never did it, so his job changed to fetching things.

"Darling Brody, you need to learn the importance of immediacy," said my mother when she demoted him.

I dry the woman off as quickly as I can, dress her in a tracksuit and push her into her chair in the corner.

I suppose I had better feed her. Looking through the cupboards, I find some cereal and a bowl. I stir the cereal and the milk together so that the cereal is soggy and kneel in front of her, spooning it into her mouth and scraping her chin with the edge of the spoon.

After breakfast, I hang the washing out, taking the woman with me.

The back garden is about double the size of a normal suburban block. The Hills Hoist is at the very back. I can just see the metal end poking out behind a trellis of creepers.

On the way to the clothesline, the woman falls over and scrapes her knee. Prickles is winding around her legs. When she falls she makes an "oomph" noise. She sits on her bum looking down at her knee. I look at her face, waiting for some pain to register, but she doesn't seem to be surprised or distressed or hurt.

I drag her back inside by the arm to inspect the wound, eager to put my first aid training into action. I'm considering a splint but then decide that it would be over the top.

I'm looking down at her leg when I notice, with increasing dread, a dark stain spreading down the inside of her tracksuit leg. She's wet herself again.

So, I put her in the bath again. She's in the bath and the phone rings. So, I run out of the bathroom and just as I'm about to pick it up, it stops.

I take her clothes out of the bathroom and put them in the washing machine. I don't know what I'd do without this washing machine.

Prickles is following me around and getting under my feet and meowing loudly, so I put him outside, but two seconds later, there he is under my feet, because I left the window open to let him come in and out as he chooses.

I put some dry food in his bowl. He sniffs at it with disdain and then starts meowing at me again. So, I reach into the cupboard and pull out a tin of stinky cat food, open it and put it in the stinky bowl. He eats it.

I go searching through the cupboards trying to find some bedclothes. The linen cupboard is neatly organized. There are sheets and pillowcases still in their original packaging. One shelf is full of handbags.

As I make the woman's bed, I notice the thick, soft texture of the sheets. Our sheets at home are thinner and more coarse.

Hearing the washing machine purr to a stop, I take the washing out. Halfway to the clothesline I find the first basket of washing that I didn't put out because of the woman's knee. *It's all too much, Toto.* So, I'm trying to get to the clothesline carrying two baskets of washing.

It was at this point that I had my first encounter with my new neighbor. When she spoke I thought that she was speaking a different language, and she was, after a fashion. I come from a long line of suits who articulate with masterly precision (except, of course, for Nanna, who refers to young men "taking their ferret for a run" and hoots at men on construction sites—usually at the same time; Nanna has no shame).

I hear a voice off to my left.

"Looks like ya gotcherands full, mate."

I look up. Through the shrubbery I can see the next-door neighbor's back veranda. It's about a meter off the ground. There's a woman standing in front of an aluminum screen door with one hand on her hip, smoking a cigarette.

"Beg yours?" I say, frowning.

She's wearing one of those flattering flannel nighties in lime with what looks like a rosebud pattern, and so I immediately don't like her.

I have never been a big fan of the nightie. The main issue that I have yet to resolve is this: how do you get into bed without the nightie sliding up and bunching around the waist? I have tried countless methods, including pulling the bedclothes to one side and rolling onto the bed sideways, but the rolling action has a sort of wringing effect, so you end up uncomfortable longways instead of sideways. It is not possible, in my experience, to get into bed with the full-length nightie on without such strenuous exercise that it will leave you puffed and wide awake.

Now, I will concede that in the confines of one's own property one should be entitled to wear whatever one pleases without judgment or discrimination. However, the lady next door must have *purchased* said nightie at some stage and one can assume that the purchasing occurred beyond the boundary of the property. Who buys a lime nightie? Not the sort of person with whom I'm likely to get along, that's who!

"I was just saying you got your hands full, mate."

"Yes. I do."

"I'm not talking about the washing, mate." She takes a drag of her cigarette between sentences and talks through a cloud of smoke. The original dragon lady—boom, boom.

I look over the vast piles of washing in my arms. "Oh?"

"Eyemeaner."

"Eyemeaner?"

"Er!" She points back toward the house with her cigarette. "Er, arya deaf?"

"Oh, you mean her."

"Yeah, mate, her. She givingyardtimeyet?"

I'm doing the translation in my head as we go along, *giving you a hard time yet*. This means there's a couple of seconds delay before I am able to respond.

"No, not really."

She takes a long drag on the cigarette. "Well, I don't reckon yoolafta wait long, yoonowdameen?"

"Pardon? Oh! You-know-what-I-mean."

"What?"

"You said 'you know what I mean.' "

"Yeah?" She cocks her head on the side and takes another drag. "You a nuffytooarya?"

"A nuffytooarya?"

"Christ! Two of yous! Just as bad as echutha."

"No, I'm the carer."

"What?"

Ccrck, are you receiving, lime nightie woman? Over, ccrck.

"Carer, you know. I look after her."

"How old arya? Twelve? Pretty poor fuckin' choice if you ask me, mate."

And with that she flicks her cigarette into the garden, spits, and walks back into her house, slamming the screen door behind her.

Well, I understood that!

Charming.

I carry the baskets to the washing line and hang out the clothes and the linen. I'm humming to myself. Something is nagging at the back of my mind. I must be hungry.

So now it's lunchtime and I make myself a sandwich. I'm looking for your plain ordinary condiment in the fridge. There are mustards: tarragon mustard, honey mustard, red peppercorn mustard. There are jellies: rosemary jelly, thyme jelly, red currant jelly. There is something called *nasi goreng*. I have a quick sniff and decide that it is probably not suitable for a sandwich.

There is a series of sun-dried vegetables: sun-dried tomatoes, sun-dried capsicum, sun-dried aubergine. Then there are several jars of tapenade. What in heaven's name is a tapenade? Where's the Vegemite?

I drag out a jar of nutmeg honey. What's wrong with ordinary squeezable honey? I spread the nutmeg honey on the bread and cut it into little triangles—force of habit.

I'm sitting out on the back step eating my sandwich. Something's nagging at me. What is it?

After lunch I sit on the couch and I'm exhausted. I pick up a magazine on the table and read that for a little while. I've done two loads of washing and I'm exhausted. Then it's time to bring it all back in again. Quickly, in case I run into that lime nightie woman next door again.

I'm standing at the washing line singing a little song.

The Grace woman! I've left her in the bath!

I run back to the house and into the bathroom. She is lying there in the bath. The bubbles have all disappeared. Most of the water has drained out of the bath. She lies there with her hands folded neatly over her belly. Her lips are blue and the skin on her hands and feet is puckered.

I can see her blue veins, like tiny vines, under the white skin of her chest and breasts. Her wet hair is wrapped in thin tendrils around her neck and across her cheek. She looks dead.

I've killed her. It's my first day and I've killed her.

I felt that cold paralyzed feeling, exactly like you get when you're watching a horror movie and you know something really scary is about to happen, but you can't look away. Except it wasn't deliciously scary, it was the real thing.

I've killed her. I'm a murderer. What do you do when you've killed someone? Do you call the police first, or the ambulance?

Then her eyes slid toward me, not blinking, cold and dry, like lizard's eyes. She held my gaze for just a moment, her lizard's eyes looking right through me, accusing.

My God, she's in there.

She's looking at me like a real person, but not. Her eyes are on mine but there's nothing. Is there? I'm *frightened* of her.

I'm holding my breath. Fright steals through my veins and it's cold. I'm frozen. My heart *ka-thump, ka-thump*s in my ears. Then her eyes slide away again.

My breath comes out in a big whoosh and I jolt into action, grabbing her by the arm and hauling her out of the bath. I dry her off as quickly as possible, by wrapping the towel around her and patting at it.

She shivers in the towel.

"I'm sorry," I say to her, rubbing her shoulders under the towel. "I forgot. I won't do it again."

She just stands there with her teeth chattering, holding the towel up to her chin with one puckered hand.

The nurse came in the afternoon for the Grace woman's physiotherapy. She's one of those no-nonsense Aussie women. She arrives and she's smoking! Can you believe it? I mean, how many little blackened gooey pieces of lung have you got to see coughed up when you're a nurse?

The nurse is lean and tall with long stick legs. Her name is Jan. She has thin lips and short curly hair. She calls me "darl."

I'm going to go to uni. I have four days left until first semester starts.

Uni is a nice stroll through the park and then a short bus trip. As I walk onto the grounds I am completely disoriented. There are tall buildings and squat buildings between the trees. It's so *big*. People are wandering about looking comfortable and relaxed. I walk quickly so that I look as if I know where I am going.

I find the library and some of my lecture theaters. "Theater" is what they look like—rows and rows and rows of chairs.

I sit in one of the chairs in the empty lecture theater. This is what I do now. I come here. No more school. No more coming home to newspaper ponchos.

My life is different now. I've made some big decisions and carried them all through with very little discomfort. It seems too simple.

Then what happens after that? I'll get a job, I suppose. Another opportunity will fall in my lap and I'll take it. Then before long I'll be thirty. The sun will continue to rise and set. Christmas will hurtle around again and again, and then I'll be dead.

I look around at the empty chairs in the lecture theater and all of a sudden this whole living business seems a bit pointless.

I think I might be having a quarter-life crisis.

● ● ●

Mr. Preston was at the house when I arrived home, and Jan the nurse had gone. I asked him what sort of changes I'm supposed to be observing in Grace.

What if, say, I leave her in a cold bath for the best part of a day and then find her staring at me like a zombie?

"I don't know what to look for," I told him.

"Well, let's not kid ourselves thinking that Grace is just going to wake up one morning and be back to her old self. We are talking about some pretty serious damage here."

Is that relief I feel?

"The capacity of the human body to heal is an amazing thing. I mean, even the doctors can't tell us how much she thinks or hears. She could still be in there. I'm certain that Grace is fighting to get out. If there's a way out, Grace will find it. She can be very persistent, believe me."

Mr. Preston smiled. He cocked his head, looking contemplative. "You know, sometimes I've been here with her talking and I think she's listening to me. She may turn her head or move her hand just a little bit. Then I think maybe it's just because I so much want her to be listening to me."

Does she stare at you? Does she give you the heebies?

He took a deep breath. "Anyway, I came here to bring you this." Mr. Preston put an answering machine on the table. "I tried to ring this morning, but there was no answer."

I smiled weakly.

"Also, I wanted to tell you about her likes and dislikes. She hates the next-door neighbors but she likes their dog. She loves her cat. She likes freshly brewed coffee, not instant. She likes real butter, not margarine. She likes tomatoes, but not cucumber. She likes soup, fresh, not tinned. She doesn't like tuna, but she does like salmon. Fresh, not tinned."

I'm thinking to myself, what is this? What's going on here? I mean, salmon? I'm not slaving over a hot stove for this woman! I don't slave over a hot stove for myself! What's next? Softly poached quail eggs?

"I won't be cooking her any salmon."

"That's a great pity," said Mr. Preston. "She is a very big fan of salmon."

"Look, can't she just eat what I eat?"

"That depends on what you eat."

So I find myself writing down a list of what the Grace woman likes and doesn't like. I tell you, poached quail eggs weren't far wrong. This is a woman with very discerning taste. Nothing tinned—especially asparagus. What a shame.

I personally think tins are the greatest, next to anything "cook in the bag." You can always just pile it up in the middle of a big plate and call it contemporary Australian cuisine.

"How does she feel about peanut butter on toast?" I inquire.

"I have never had her opinion either way regarding peanut butter on toast. But on the whole, I think I can safely say that she would prefer pâté if there were a choice."

Great. This is all I need.

"You seem to know a lot about your client's tastes." I was a bit sharp—but then "chef" wasn't in the job description.

I have mental images of myself trying to prepare finnan haddie and weeping and singing "Somewhere Over the Rainbow" and looking down at Prickles saying, "This is all too much, Toto."

Mr. Preston smiles at me, looking sad again. "Grace is more than a client. She is also a dear, dear friend."

• • •

That's all very well, but in bed at night, alone, I have to remind myself that she is a dear, dear friend and not a monster.

When I was younger I used to share a bedroom with my little brother, Brody. We had double bunks. He used to laugh in his sleep. I think back now and I'm guessing that he was just a happy child who had happy dreams, but then it was the creepiest thing. He used to make this eerie gurgling noise. It was freaky.

I would lie in bed frozen in fear, with my eyes wide open looking at the slats above me, absolutely certain that my brother had been replaced by an evil goblin who was up there just waiting and laughing about evil goblin things.

At night, now, I lie rigid in bed, straining my ears, like I used to when I shared a room with Brody. I hear a thump from the lounge room and my muscles seize. It's just the cat, of course, jumping down from the windowsill. I can hear the very tips of his claws ticking across the wooden floor.

I keep seeing her lizard's eyes in my mind. They slide toward me over and over. In my imagination her dead eyes turn toward me and I can hear her speak.

You left me here to drown.

At night, alone, she is a zombie—alive but dead inside.

The floor in this old house creaks. A branch scrapes slowly back and forth across the roof of the veranda. The house is old and I wonder if anybody has ever died in this room.

Why worry about old ghosts when there is one still very much alive in the next room?

This room is not completely dark. Streetlights screened by moving foliage make indecipherable shapes and shadows of the furniture. I can imagine her standing in the doorway to my room—dull eyes in a white face, moist lips drooping loosely.

I get up and move the distressed dressing table across the doorway.

i wake up and see the dressing table pressed up against the doorway and feel like a complete dill. There are scratches on the floor where I have dragged it.

The Grace woman is lying in her bed looking about as malevolent as your average lop-eared bunny.

I am a nutbag.

I manage to get her to the toilet early on, avoiding the linen- and clothes-washing cycle of yesterday. I need to shop, so I dress her and we shuffle down the street.

I have hold of the Grace woman by the sleeve of her shirt. She walks very slowly and I have to keep dragging at her arm to make her keep up.

It's hot for late February—hot and humid. The sun is

beaming down like a spotlight through the hole in the ozone layer. I can almost feel my skin being gently grilled.

I'm picking out the rented houses as I'm walking along the street. I think if the grass on the front lawn is more than knee height the property is rented. Across the road I spy a nanna with a big spade vigorously attacking a long weedy tentacle that has crept through her side fence.

There are cats on almost every second veranda. This is a very pro-cat neighborhood. They lie with their paws tucked primly under their chests. Gangs of mynah birds are screaming at them from nearby trees. You can see the pupils of the cats' eyes expanding and contracting like a missile sight.

Mynah birds are the homeys of the bird world. You can hear them in the trees, saying in bird, "Yo! Yo! Wha's up wit you, man! You wanna piece of me, man? Don't go dissin' my posse, or we gonna kick some ass, you know what I'm sayin'?" There are no native birds around here, they have all been driven away by the mynah birds and their gang violence.

I have to go to the greengrocer and the deli to purchase all the "must-have" gourmet items for the Grace woman's daily cuisine. *It's all too much, Toto.*

While I am in the deli the Italian lady, all smiles, says, "Good morning, chicken. Can I kkhelp you?" in a really strong accent. I say in return, "No thanks, I'm just grazing." I meant browsing but she was kind enough not to pick me up on it.

Looking around, I see that blueberries are on special. They're selling a whole box of punnets for nine dollars. It occurs to me that if I had a family to feed and I didn't have much money I could buy a whole box of whatever was on special and pretend that it was a party. I've never thought of us as poor. Maybe we are? I smiled as I thought about it. Mother has never made us feel poor.

The main street is great. There are all these ancient Italian men grouped on street corners waving their arms about vigorously. This suburb is like a Mafia retirement village.

There are funky twenty-somethings in crisp white shirts and dark glasses, sipping lattes in street cafés, talking on mobile phones. There are herbals wandering about in tie-dyed cheesecloth nibbling at uncomfortable-looking lip rings. There are Goths sweating. It's too hot for Goths to be out and about, but even Goths have to do their grocery shopping sometime.

Everybody here is wearing a costume. It's a parade. This is very different from home, where everyone is dressed in "drab"—whether suits or overalls. At home they are all struggling desperately to conform.

I come from a small place where everybody wants to be the same. Everybody tries to think the same. They band together in ferocious solidarity. Through similarity they bond. Now, here I am where the people unite in their difference—"We are all different from each other," they cry collectively.

Or maybe they are all pro-cat? "We come from across the globe, we are different ages and have different beliefs, BUT we all choose to spend our lives with cats. We are as one on the whole cat issue!"

My friend Amanda is coming out of a real estate agent's office as the Grace woman and I shuffle past. We were quite good friends at school, but I haven't seen her for a few months. We are proximity friends. All of our conversations have been location-based. Besides, Amanda is a rosella, and being a sparrow, I don't even comprehend her world.

She leans forward to hug me, but I'm not the hugging type so I step back. She catches me by the upper arms, squeezing and shaking and smiling. We are experiencing that uncomfortable moment when there's physical contact. This is why I am not a hugger.

Amanda's getting married. While she's talking she's darting her eyes at the Grace woman as if she were trying to include her in the conversation.

Amanda is getting married to Bozza, the Neanderthal tiler. She sounds so smug, but I can't think what she has to be smug about. She's waggling her left hand in front of my face, showing me her engagement ring and looking coy.

"Haven't you got a boyfriend yet?" she says, with such pity. I'm just waiting for her to say *Oh well, there are plenty of fish in the sea* or some other appalling cliché. She thinks that getting married is the ultimate goal, and assumes that I do as well.

I choose not to be irritated. Actually, I feel sorry for Amanda marrying Bozza. His real name is Rick, but everyone calls him Bozza. Bozza's the name of a man with a bright future. History is absolutely littered with great Bozzas—Sir Bozza, General Bozza, King Bozza the Magnificent.

Amanda has always been a really pretty girl. She has long blond hair and olive skin, and she blushes a charming, soft, peachy glow across the cheeks (not like the big, bright red, iridescent, lighthouse-strength beam that my moon face emits).

She's also really smart. I always thought she'd get over Bozza and have some kind of career. I thought she'd be sitting at the street cafés sipping lattes with some brooding dark man in a suit.

I could never understand why she liked "Bozza" anyway. I mean, he was good-looking in Year 9, but now that he's getting older he's put on a bit of weight, and the sullen, cool look doesn't really fit with bulgy jowls. And he's still not very smart.

I think it's that thing that women do where they try to "fix" a man. They find some rowdy dropkick and say, "But he's really sweet on the inside." They try to fix a man a bit like renovating a house. They find a handyman's dream (ideally with "ocean glimpses") and try to renovate.

I'm eighteen and know everything—well, not *everything*, but I do know, for example, that leopards rarely change their spots on command. They may sport a nice tartan shawl, if pressed, but earnest spot-changing requires some considerable desire and willpower on the part of the leopard in question.

Amanda has definitely turned out to be a renovator, but I haven't seen that much change. The only thing that's different is that Amanda doesn't call him Bozza anymore; she doesn't even call him Rick. Now she calls him Richard. It's just like slapping a coat of paint on a tin shed and calling it a cabana.

●　　●　　●

It turns out that I'm not the only one who can glow a raspberry-colored glow. The Grace woman got sunburned today. I'll have to remember to put sunscreen on her before we go out. I smear her face in aloe vera and she sits in her wingback chair looking as if she has a shiny red cue ball for a head.

The red light is flashing on the answering machine and I listen to the message.

"Gracey, it's Yvonne. I know it's been forever. One puts these things off and before you know it, it's been so long that you can't bring yourself to phone. I know you're cross, because I didn't even get a Christmas card. You're not allowed to be cross because you haven't phoned either. I'm being the brave one. Now it's your turn. Please call me back."

I suppose the Yvonne person doesn't know what has happened. I press the Delete button.

Flicking through the Grace woman's CDs, I put on some cool jazz. Most of the CDs are "jazz to sip lattes by." I wonder if she used to have breakfast in those street cafés?

I put on a white shirt and some red lipstick so I fit in with the music. I feel almost funky for a moment.

I cook some pasta sprinkled with shaved Parmesan. I mush up the woman's with a fork and feed her, squatting down in front of her chair. She chews with her mouth open and looks blankly over my shoulder. I can see pasta mush gathering at the corners of her mouth. I watch the food rolling around her mouth with a nauseated fascination. I give her a drink of water and she holds the glass in two hands, like a child. I take it from her, trying not to touch the Parmesan goo that has accumulated around the rim.

I serve my dinner piled up on a big white plate and eat it outside (CAC *al fresco*, darling).

I sit in the lovely outdoor area out the back that's all paved and has terra-cotta pots filled with herbs and fruit trees. There's a lion-head fountain on the wall by a little pond. I find a tap under some creeping vines and the water starts to trickle out of the lion's mouth.

It is very pleasant to sit out here while the sun goes down, listening to the jazz and the fountain.

Well, it's pleasant until the neighbors start fighting. There's a lot of swearing. I walk back inside and watch telly instead.

Half an hour later I hear a noise outside. I pull the curtain back just in time to see the bloke from next door lay a boot into their dog's belly. The dog sprawls across the lawn and then scampers yelping down the garden.

Ah, so they are *dog people*. They are not with the rest of the neighborhood on the whole cat issue.

I can see the confusion in the dog's little brown eyes as he peeks out from under the oleander bush. I feel hot anger rising up inside me. I hate people who hurt animals.

The bloke from next door turns around and sees me watching him. He sticks his middle finger up at me and then stalks back into his house.

Charming.

When I go to bed I pull the distressed dressing table across the doorway again. I tell myself that it's to give me some notice if she tries to come into my room, but it's a lie.

Lying in the dark, I have an image of her dragging herself over the dressing table and toward me with her unblinking lizard's eyes, and that's somehow worse. It's an image of malice and intent that is undeserved. I feel guilty, but not guilty enough to move the dressing table back again.

Mr. Preston took the Grace woman shopping today so that I could go to the uni to buy books and things.

My mother rang as I was leaving.

"Mum, are we poor?"

She was quiet for a moment. "Why do you ask that?"

"Well, I've never really thought about groceries before, but now I have to shop and so I know how expensive things are and I saw blueberries on special," I replied.

I could tell she was choosing her words carefully. "We may not be as fiscally robust as others. Certainly, I have been better off in the past, but things change and you roll with it. You have always had a roof over your head and food in your bellies. I have always made sure you were happy and healthy. One does the best that one can, and that's all anyone can ask of you."

"Oh," I said. She was becoming defensive and that wasn't my intent.

"Besides, riches and success are all to do with your goals. My goal is for both of you to be happy and be able to take advantage of opportunities as they arise and you are and you can. So I am a success. There now."

Have another lychee.

•   •   •

Buying textbooks is a very harrowing experience. Not only do I have to spend all the money that I had saved up over Christmas, but also I know that I have to absorb everything in those books within the next fourteen weeks.

When I got home I plonked all the books on my desk. I could hear Mr. Preston in the lounge room singing along to something by Ella Fitzgerald and Louis Armstrong.

Mr. Preston was dancing with Grace.

Will I find when we meet again,
The glamour, the glory still aglow.

Mr. Preston was whirling Grace around the lounge room. He's quite light on his feet for a big man. I sat down on the lounge to watch them. Grace was staring blankly at Mr. Preston's chest, one hand draped over his shoulder. I looked down at her feet. Sometimes he would lift her off the floor and spin her around. I thought I could see her feet moving, even anticipating the steps that Mr. Preston was going to make.

Mr. Preston was singing, loudly, and badly, but he was taking great care, leading her very gently and lifting her up when she missed a step. She looked very small in his arms.

On her feet were shiny red patent leather shoes, square-toed with a wedged heel. Beautiful shoes.

When they'd finished, I clapped, and Mr. Preston bowed. "Thank you very much, my dear. You see, our Grace is quite a mover."

He gently lowered Grace into her chair. "Dancing is the best way to wear in a pair of new shoes, I always say."

"They're lovely shoes."

"Yes, they are. Grace has always loved shoes, haven't you, my dear?"

He clapped his hands together, beaming at me. "Care for a glass of wine?"

I walked into the kitchen and fetched two wineglasses while Mr. Preston opened a bottle of wine.

"Will you not have a glass?" asked Mr. Preston from behind me.

I turned to face him. He was smiling at me. He had the two glasses in his hands. I was confused. "Isn't one of those for me?"

"No, this is Grace's glass."

"You're not going to give her alcohol!"

"Why not?"

Because she can't control herself. Because she's at our mercy. Because she has no choice. It's like giving wine to a baby.

"Well, it's not right."

He handed me one of the glasses. "Taste this."

I took a sip.

He frowned at me. "This is a very good wine."

I don't really know anything about wine but I liked this one. It had a sort of buttery taste. "Yes, it's very good," I responded, wanting to sound as if I knew what I was talking about.

"What hideous crime has she committed?" Mr. Preston asked me.

"Pardon?"

"I'm asking you, what hideous crime has Grace committed that she should for all eternity be condemned to never tasting a great wine?" He held my gaze for a moment and then took the glass from my hand and carried it over to where Grace was sitting leaned over staring at her new shoes.

"You know, I think you are the most bright, vivacious and exciting person I have ever met."

I whirled around, banging the cupboard door shut. If he thought there was going to be some sort of Sean Connery/Michael Douglas type of action happening here, then he was *wrong*. He—he didn't even know me!

I was just about to open my mouth and say so when I realized he was talking to Grace.

"Ever since I have known you, you have always chosen the best of things for yourself. I have watched you for many years. In all things, you always savored textures: creamy Camembert, fresh light cotton, rich dark chocolate, soft wool. But the thing you have always enjoyed most was a full dry white.

"You would sit on this chair or out on the veranda with one foot tucked under you and sip a glass of wine. You would take small sips and roll it over your taste buds, telling stories, listening to this music, laughing or quietly watching the sun go down." He handed her the glass. "I hope this meets with your approval."

I wondered again what their relationship was, before. He took an unusual amount of interest in her care for a lawyer. But he's not her husband, otherwise he would live here. Besides, he touches her tentatively. He's comfortable with a certain degree of familiarity, but not like a person who is touching someone with whom there is real physical intimacy. He touches her like a brother or a cousin. And this is a house clearly arranged for one. This house is feminine. Grace was single.

"Were you in love with her?"

Mr. Preston looked up at me sharply. I was reminded of the look my grandfather (Nanna's "hubby") used to give me when I asked a personal question. Grandpa would give me that look and then he'd say, "And how're you off for socks and jocks then, hmm?"

Mr. Preston had this look on his face as if he was going to ask me how I was off for socks and jocks. His eyes were screwed up a little. There was a tenseness between us.

"I mean, that's a pretty personal observation, that's all. It sounds as if you were in love with her." I was embarrassed and I could feel a blush coming on, so I turned and opened the cupboard door again, pretending to look for something.

When I looked out again he was smiling. The tenseness was gone. "Everyone was a little bit in love with Grace."

He stood up and walked over to where I was standing against the kitchen bench. "You know, it's only now that I can tell her things that I've always wanted to say. I was always afraid that she would . . ."

Crawl over the dressing table in the middle of the night with lizard's eyes?

He shifted on his feet. "You see, Grace had this way of belittling people. Insult was an art form for Grace. Over the years she had perfected it. I just never wanted to be on the receiving end of that abuse."

"Is that why you're here? Is that why you do this—the wine and shoes and everything? Because you were in love with her?"

Mr. Preston shifted on his feet again. I was overstepping the mark this time. But he answered anyway.

"I owe Grace. I would never have got as far in my career, in my life, if it weren't for her. In a lot of ways I had the career that she should have had. I didn't recognize it at the time—the unfairness of it. See, that was her other skill—getting you to do things by making you think it was your own idea. She was a master manipulator."

He paused for a moment. I realized that with the pause the opportunity to find out more was gone, for the time being, anyway. The conversation was gently steered in another direction.

"I see the way people treat Grace. I see her sisters coming in here and taking away her beautiful things—things she so carefully collected over the years. I see nurses and carers speaking to her as if she's some kind of slow child. I hear people talking about her as if she isn't in the room."

I frowned, and looked in toward the lounge room where Grace was sitting. "Like you are now?"

"I'm trying to tell you something. Pay attention." He frowned at me and paused to make sure I was listening.

"I went to see her in the hospital and I watched them shoveling tasteless pureed muck into her face."

Just like I have been.

"Grace was just sitting slumped in a chair with *slippers* on. It was so ugly. There was no dignity, there was no life— no grace. Here was this exquisite, intelligent woman sitting there in slippers with pulpy gray slop dribbling down her chin. It was obscene."

He was standing with his hands on his hips, frowning at me. I could see anger in his face.

"I don't know how much she can feel or understand. I don't know whether she still thinks or dreams, but I have to give her the benefit of the doubt. There have been times when she has been unkind or cruel, but . . ."

Mr. Preston shook his head slowly.

"Can you imagine a worse hell than being humiliated and pitied for the rest of your life? Grace, who delighted in music and in wine and food and literature and art and sur- rounded herself with beauty and light."

He circled around with his hand palm up.

"If you knew Grace then, you'd know that nothing could be more offensive, nothing could be more abhorrent to her than spending the rest of her life this way."

Mr. Preston looked tired and old.

"If I can in some small way alleviate that pain, if I can in some small way give her something like a shadow, a hint, a scent on the breeze of pleasure and, and—well, of *life*. That's why I do this, I'm trying to give her a spark. I'm try- ing to give her back a sweet taste of her life—her old life. Do you understand?"

He was looking at me intently.

"I think that's why I chose you. You have life in you. When I saw you, I thought that you had that spark. It's very important to me that you understand. It's very important for Grace."

I looked over to where Grace was sitting with one leg under the other. Prickles was on her lap again. She was looking out the window. She was resting the wineglass on the arm of the chair. Sitting there in her shiny new shoes, she might have been mistaken for an ordinary person. She might have been a very wealthy ordinary person—with a maid.

This morning we have been blessed with a visit from two of Grace's sisters.

Tight Mouth is Brioney. There is another one called Angelica but she lives somewhere far away and doesn't visit except at Christmas.

The woman with the rubber gloves, her name is Charity. She's about as charitable as Saddam Hussein.

Charity is glad Angelica doesn't visit more often, because "her husband owns a car dealership and she dresses up like a tart and thinks she's better than everybody."

Anyway, they "just popped in to see how things are settling in." Also wondering what sort of hours I was working, and whether there was anything that was in the way?

I explain that I'm settling in well, that I'm working all the time and that everything is just fine where it is, thank you very much.

Tight Mouth Brioney, with the Beatles haircut, is in legal administration (prison warden?) and teaches something called "quilling" at a community college.

What do you suppose quilling is, then? I guess that it's somewhere between fletching and quilting, and carry on with the conversation as though I'm up on arts and crafts. She's one of those tall, big-boned women with a long neck. Her long neck is even more noticeable because she has no chin. She looks like something, but I can't put my finger on it.

Rubber Gloves Charity is short and podgy. She has three incredibly bright and talented children, Jeremy, Bianca and Simone. I nod and smile but I'm not really listening. She's one of those people who talks to the ceiling, so I don't think she notices. She also fluffs her hair while she's talking.

Brioney explains to me while Charity is "powdering her nose" that Charity's husband is a crook who's probably going to end up in the clink and that her children are totally spoilt. She doesn't whisper but talks in a low voice and nods gravely when she finishes a sentence. While she's talking I'm looking at her head.

What does she look like?

According to Brioney, Charity never got her figure back after having babies and it's probably too late now. She says she thinks I should understand that the relationship between Charity and Angelica has been strained because Angelica has a perfect figure and Charity is jealous. *Grave nod.*

She also tells me that there's a good solarium at her gym and I should go there and "get a bit of color to me."

I was going to explain that if I went to a solarium I would get blisters and spend the rest of the day frequently passing out. I have very sensitive skin. I was going to tell her that, at best, all I can get is a bit of a beige. I think better of it and just smile instead. People who tan don't understand people who don't, in the same way that people who enjoy jogging don't understand people who don't. Jogging is another activity that gives me blisters and makes me pass out.

Charity whisks me out the back while Brioney makes a cup of coffee and tells me that Brioney is living in sin with a lazy man who gambles and that he's never going to make an honest woman of her because she won't do the simple things, like cooking a decent meal, that make a man happy.

She talks in one of those hissy whispery voices with her eyes very wide. She puts her hand on my forearm as she talks so I can't get away.

She tells me that there's a lot of fuss these days about women's rights, and of course she's all for it, *but* there are more women than men and if you want a good one, sometimes you have to compromise a little bit on your feminist ideals.

She tells me that I shouldn't wait too long to have children because they're such treasures and if I don't have kids soon I'll end up old and lonely like Brioney.

She also tells me that she feels I should understand that the relationship between herself and Angelica has been strained recently and it has nothing to do with weight, whatever Brioney thinks about it.

They both explained to me in front of Grace in normal

voices that they felt it was a tragic thing that happened to Grace because she was so successful in her career and everything, but they had always secretly thought that she only got as far as she did "because she wore short skirts, if you get my meaning." *Grave nod, wide eyes.*

They made furtive glances in Grace's general direction as though they were afraid she might stand up and dispute the matter.

Because I am eighteen I know a great many things; for example, I know that sticks and stones are indeed very effective mechanisms with which to break bones; however, a few poorly aimed (or sadly, well-aimed) words can have someone's metaphorical eye out and therefore one ought not wave one's words about willy-nilly.

I told Grace when Brioney and Charity left that I thought her sisters were a pair of gossipy old cows and I hoped they would never come back.

● ● ●

Jan arrives in the early afternoon for Grace's physio. My first lecture is tonight. I'm very nervous.

I walk through the park with my bag on my back and a fresh, bright, new notepad under my arm.

There are several exercise areas with wooden equipment and a sign that tells you what you are supposed to do. I have a turn at the balance beam. It's only about a foot off the ground, but I'm pretending it's the high wire at the circus.

I'm trying to do a drumroll, but I sound more like an out-of-balance ceiling fan, so I do the *Jaws* suspense music instead.

I'm thinking it's weird beginning the day at seven o'clock in the night.

I'm really looking forward to starting university. I'm a nerd. I'm not ashamed. I have a passion for science fiction. I've had braces. I put up my hand to answer questions. I go to the library. I even peek through my textbooks before the start of term.

So, I get to the university. There is a huge car park at the front the size of about two football fields, and two paths going down through the buildings. I pick the closest one. There are trees everywhere and students lying about on the grass slapping themselves.

I'm walking down the path to the lecture theater. I'm early, as every self-respecting nerd should be. There are a few other nerds waiting here too. They're slapping themselves.

Why are they slapping themselves?

I put my bag down at my feet and tighten the jumper I've got tied around my waist. I slap my forearm.

Mosquitoes!

A little cloud of mosquitoes circles lazily around me.

The door to the lecture theater opens and people start to come out. I choose a seat up front and I put all my fresh, bright, new colored pens out on the little half-table in front of me.

The first thing the lecturer tells us is that he's going to have the pleasure of the company of at least seventy percent of us for the same course this time next year, because that's the failure rate.

"Not I," says the nerd.

We have a halftime break. All the other students file out to go to the toilet, or smoke, or chat to each other. I sit at my little desk, underlining the key phrases in purple and turning my bullet points into cheery little stars. I've always taken great pride in my notes.

After the break, the lecturer puts up the dates of all the assignments and the chapters we are supposed to have read. I take down the dates and cross-reference them into my diary.

At the end of the lecture an Asian bloke approaches me. He's smiling and he's nodding. He's got long, thick black hair tied at the nape of his neck.

I think he says something about can he borrow my notes because he doesn't speak English very well, he's only been here for a short while and he can't keep up with the lecturer. I think he said his name was Hiro, but that could well have been part of the explanation.

I can feel an enormous radioactive blush coming on, because I can't understand what he's saying, and for some reason I'm finding that intensely embarrassing.

I can feel the redness rising up my neck and my chin first. Just my neck and chin. Everything else is a nice ordinary ivory. So I pull my collar up to my bottom lip. I'm nodding at him and smiling, like suddenly pulling your shirt up over half your face is a perfectly ordinary way to behave.

The blush has crept up the back of my neck and over my scalp to my ears. I push my chin out to keep the collar of my shirt over my chin while I let go with my hand. I'm undoing the jumper around my waist. I drop the collar and quickly wrap my jumper over my head so the collar reaches down to my eyebrows and the sleeves are wrapped loosely around my neck.

Every self-respecting nerd carries a jumper, even in the

height of summer. Every nerd knows it's important to be prepared for any eventuality.

I think he's telling me that he'll find me and give the notes back to me in the next day or two. I don't really know. I'm not concentrating on what he's saying. I'm blush-entranced.

The blush is creeping down my temples and across my cheeks and since I can't put the jumper over my whole face and still maintain even a shred of dignity, I look intently over Hiro's shoulder instead.

I'm thinking to myself (safe now that I'm looking at something else, therefore he can't see the blush, good old Rachel logic in action) that Hiro is going to run off with my bright, fresh, new notepad with each paragraph written in a different bright, fresh, new color and I'll never see him again. But since it's got only one lot of notes in it (and I'm a nerd who is excited about learning so I've already memorized it all anyway), I give the notes to him. He walks backward away from me still smiling and nodding.

He's got really square shoulders. They don't slope down at all. They're very nice shoulders.

I'm not going to be able to do any revision tonight. I'm leaving the university now with my jumper still over my head and not looking at anyone who walks past me. It takes a while for one of these really intense blushes to subside.

My mother phones me as soon as I walk in the door.

"How was it? How did it go?"

"Oh, you know. It was OK."

"Stop being so teenage," she replies.

"OK then, it was pretty good. I sat down. A man talked. I came home."

"And did you make any friends?" she asks.

"Yeah, there was a guy. He borrowed my notes."

"Are you sure that's a good idea?"

"It'll be fine."

I tell Mum about Hiro and the blush. She thinks it's funny. I can imagine her standing in the kitchen with her hand on her belly while she throws back her head laughing.

Next to the phone there is an address book. Flicking through the pages, I see the number for the Yvonne person. I punch in the numbers and listen to the dial tone.

"Hello?"

"Is this Yvonne?" I ask.

"Yes, who is this?"

"You don't know me. My name is Rachel. I'm Grace's carer. You rang for her yesterday. The reason she hasn't called you back is that she's brain-damaged."

There is a pause on the line.

"Are you still there?" I ask.

The voice that answers me is choked.

"Oh God, I can't believe it."

"Yes. Anyway, I just thought I'd let you know," I say.

"Thank you," says the voice, and then the line goes dead.

i took Grace for a walk this morning. She moves slowly and she's easily distracted. I think it's good for her to get some exercise.

I thought I'd take her to the beach, but I was worried she'd tire and I wouldn't be able to get her home. I can't take her long distances in the car because I've only got one snorkel.

Anyway, I smothered her in sunscreen and we walked through the park. It was a really lovely sunny day, not too hot.

We walked through the tidy park with its rotunda and play equipment painted in primary colors. The roses were in bloom, so when Grace got tired we sat under a big fig tree and I tucked some tiny yellow rosebuds in her hair.

She had her mouth closed and except for the dullness of her eyes, she almost looked pretty.

In the tidy park there is a little coffee shop, except it's not called a coffee shop, it's called a teahouse. Coffee shops are only called coffee shops, or cafés, if they are in the street. If they are in the park or anywhere else where there's a view, they're called a teahouse.

I saw Mr. Preston sitting at one of the outside tables with another man. Mr. Preston was sitting with one ankle resting on his knee, slouched back with his hands laced behind his head. The other man was dressed the same, in a dark suit and sunglasses. He was quite a bit slimmer than Mr. Preston.

Mr. Preston stood up and waved us over.

"Good morning, ladies," he said, looking intense.

"Good morning, Mr. Preston." It came out in the singsong way we used to welcome our principal in primary school. I couldn't help it! It was ingrained. Mr. Preston smiled and shifted his weight from one foot to the other, and I realized that he might have thought that I was making fun of him.

"Rachel, this is my brother, Anthony."

Anthony Preston stood up and took my hand in both of his. He didn't shake it; instead he held it for a moment. His palms were soft and dry. I couldn't see his eyes because of his sunglasses, but he had perfectly straight white teeth.

His lips turned up at the edges when he smiled. Some people's lips, when they smile, just pull back from their teeth sideways. Anthony Preston's lips definitely turned upward.

He was very good-looking. He was smiling at me in that amused way of someone who knows you're thinking they're good-looking.

He looked the same as Mr. Preston, but about five years younger and twenty kilos lighter.

"Anthony, this is Rachel, our wonderful carer, and of course you know Grace."

Anthony turned his head in Grace's direction. Then he lifted his glasses up to the top of his head and smiled at me again. His eyes were almost unnaturally blue. He held eye contact with me for just long enough for me to feel uncomfortable. The weight of his eyes felt like a physical touch. I shivered.

I've always felt uncomfortable around really good-looking people. It's as if they remind me how awkward I am. I never know what to say or how to behave.

We all stood there for a moment, not knowing what to say. Finally, Anthony said, "Won't you join us, Rachel?" He pulled out a chair next to his and sat down, patting the seat. He had a sort of hungry look in his eye that made me very self-conscious.

Mr. Preston was frowning, still standing looking at his brother. I watched as he transformed into *the large and growly bear*. "You rude, arrogant bastard," he snarled.

Anthony Preston, still smiling, turned to look at Mr. Preston, who was standing with his hands on his hips, frowning.

I didn't know what to do, so I just stood still.

Anthony Preston threw back his head and laughed

through his white teeth. "I'm sorry, I'm sorry. Won't you join us, Rachel *and Grace*."

He patted the seat next to him and then in an exaggerated movement leaned across to the next seat and patted that one as well. Then he sat back and raised both his hands up to his shoulders, palms outward.

I looked at Mr. Preston and his brother, involved in some kind of masculine power struggle.

"Umm, no. Thank you. Grace and I are walking. I, that is *we*, hope you have a pleasant afternoon."

Then I took Grace by the elbow, steering her away toward home.

i have made a discovery. I was in Grace's study and I found something. I'd just put her to bed. The last few days I've been reading before she goes to sleep, or before I do. I put her to bed, and then I sit on the bed next to her and read to her until she goes to sleep.

Sometimes I wake up dribbling on my arm. Grace is staring at the ceiling, waiting patiently for me to get on with the story. I wonder if she's thinking, "Well, I'm all for dramatic pauses, but really!"

Sometimes I've been reading in bed and fallen asleep and dropped the book on my face. Boy, that doesn't half give me a fright! *Ahh, someone just dropped a book on my face! Oh . . . it was me.*

Sometimes I do that thing where my body sort of convulses and I shock myself awake with the involuntary movement. Watching people do this is my favorite method of alleviating boredom on long train trips. I purposely sit in full view of lone passengers who look really tired, so I can have a chuckle. Especially those really respectable people dressed in fancy clothes. I just love that head-lolling-about thing, it kills me!

Anyway, I think Grace enjoys it. I mean the reading, not the convulsing or head-lolling. Her eyes rove around the room. She looks at the ceiling. After a while, she starts to blink slow, long blinks, until eventually her eyes stay closed. Then I slowly stand up and go to bed.

Sometimes I read some more in my own bed. Grace doesn't seem to notice the missed bits. Besides, she's probably read them all before anyway.

I'd just put her to bed and I walked into the study to pick a new book. I'd pulled out a few likely prospects—nothing heavy, murder mysteries mostly. I try to avoid anything that's likely to have a sex scene in it. It's the same with videos. I blush like crazy. You can see it coming a mile away, you're reading away and then all of a sudden someone starts to *feel warm skin*, or they start to notice *soft curves* about each other's persons or they start letting *soft moans* escape. I'm out of there before backs start arching. It's all too much.

I walked through the wardrobe. Grace's study is quite small. There are bookshelves on either side, going up to the ceiling. There are dictionaries, big thick tomes in different languages and law texts.

Anyway, I'd pulled out a couple of books, and then I noticed that there was something in the bookshelf, stuffed behind the books. It was an old shoe box. We'd read a few books from that shelf. How could I not have noticed it before?

I peeked back through the wardrobe to Grace's bedroom. She was lying in bed doing the long blink thing. I turned on the desk lamp and sat down with the box on the desk in front of me.

The box must have once been white, but now it was gray. The lid was crinkly and loose and the sides were bowed, as if it had been squashed.

I looked furtively through the wardrobe door again. Grace's eyes were closed and her mouth had fallen open.

This was a spooky box for sure. "Spooky box," that's a Kateism.

I went to see my friend Kate in her flat one day. She doesn't have a couch. You're supposed to sit around on big velvet cushions. Kate looks like a little elf or a fairy, sitting on a big velvet cushion with her skinny legs folded up underneath her. I just look uncomfortable and get pins and needles.

She was depressed about splitting up with Maxwell (again). Kate and Maxwell have been together since forever, but they break up for about twenty-four hours every couple of months. She laughs about it when it's not happening. But this particular time she was in the depths of despair. This time was *forever*.

Yeah, sure.

She said she'd been going through the Maxwell parts of her spooky box.

"What's a spooky box?"

"You know, the box from which you conjure your ghosts."

"I haven't got a spooky box."

"Yes you have, everyone's got a spooky box. Some people have a spooky drawer, some people have a spooky cupboard, or a spooky room. My grandma has a spooky house."

I looked into Kate's spooky box. "A train ticket," I say. "There's nothing spooky about that."

"Not for you, maybe. When I bought that ticket, Maxwell and I had been fighting all day."

Kate and Maxwell always fight all day—not that you can tell. Maxwell always stands around looking bored and surly, so it's difficult to tell if he's being grumpy or just cool.

I have always thought that Maxwell behaves like someone waiting impatiently to go somewhere else. I've had a drink with them a few times after work. Kate goes to a particular pub that is decorated with old-fashioned colonial-looking things like horse harnesses and crates and rusty farming equipment, liberally draped across every flat surface.

In *complete* contrast with the "homestead" theme, this particular pub plays ska to the exclusion of almost all other musical styles (except, of course, for reggae, which grinds alarmingly against rustic charm).

So, we went to this pub, and everyone's supercool, sort of wriggling to the music because they're too cool to dance with any vigor. Maxwell wouldn't sit down. He would stand a few meters away with his back to us, one hand in his pocket, waiting, even if it was for hours.

I found it really irritating because whenever Kate wanted to talk to him he couldn't hear her, and she'd have to say everything two or three times.

In every conversation I have ever had with him I have had the overwhelming impression that he's trying to wind up the conversation so he can leave. *How are you, Maxwell? Fine, fine (quick look at his watch).* No wonder they fight all the time. He would drive me insane.

Anyway, Kate is sitting on her velvet cushion with the contents of her spooky box in little piles on the floor in front of her. She clutches the train ticket to her bosom. "We got on that train so exhausted from yelling at each other . . ."

Maxwell yells?

". . . that we fell asleep. When we woke up, we had slept through our stop and two hours of stops after that. We ended up in this tiny little town. It was freezing cold and windy and it was six hours before the next train would come through to take us back."

Kate sighs. Her lower lip is quivering.

She's such a drama queen.

"We went to this little pub. We drank black beer. We played pool with the locals and we listened to this wizened old man. He had a face like a walnut. He must have been about a hundred. He read poetry and played the clarinet. He was one of the best performers I have ever heard in my whole life. That was one of the funnest afternoons I have ever had, even if we did get fined for fare evasion."

Then Kate started to cry. So I struggled out of my velvet cushion and left.

13

Grace was lying on her side, snoring softly now, so I wiped the dust from the top of the spooky box, took off the lid and laid it upside down on the desk.

The box was stuffed full of pieces of paper, some yellowing and wrinkly on the edges, photos in plastic sleeves, birthday cards, letters, just the sorts of things I had expected.

I felt a little bit guilty, but I picked up the first piece of paper, propped up my feet on the computer tower and read.

Dear Shouter and Screamer,

I have lived next door to you for six months now. Thank you for the time you brought in my washing when it rained. However, I have some minor objections.

One: Shouter, I object to the way you beat your dog after you have a fight with Screamer. Yes, I will admit that he is revolting and has no manners, but you have no one to blame but yourself for his odious lack of social skills and all-round offensiveness.

Two: Screamer, I'm all for equality and I am the first to stand up for women's rights, but for a woman whose parents (I assume they are your parents, they have the same dulcet and soothing tones) clean your entire house twice a week, wash your car, do your shopping and clean your clothes, is it really necessary to protest so vocally every night about having to do the dishes?

Three: Further on the dog issue. Maybe the reason he eats your flowers, your outdoor furniture, your shoes (and mine) is that he has learned that he will only ever receive attention after he behaves badly. I know this because I have only seen him happy once in your presence. He was galloping gleefully around the Hills Hoist with a now not-so-white sandshoe firmly in his teeth. You were spluttering and roaring as you ducked and weaved around on socked feet. I was amused.

My advice to you, Shouter, is to leave her, she is a witch, you will be much better off.

Screamer, just do the dishes, OK?

I feel fondness only for the dog. You don't deserve him.

I confess in advance to egging your house as I leave for work in the early hours of tomorrow morning.

Grace

The telephone rang. I figured I'd let the answering machine get it. It's me! No, actually it's Mum. We have the same voice. I need to answer that. She'll worry if I'm not here.

I could hear my own voice, but not, coming down the hall, "Are you there, Rachel darling?"

I put the lid back on the box and pushed it back in its place behind the books and shuffle down the hallway to pick up the phone. I think about telling her about the spooky box but decide not to.

I talk to Brody for a little while. That is, I talk. He grunts and then eventually he says, "You know, Rach, there's no pause on this game I'm playing. . . ."

I say, "This is relevant to me because . . ."

I love saying that. I use it at every available opportunity.

He says, "Well, it's a hired game and I only have it overnight. . . ."

I get the hint and hang up.

Brody used to be a nerd too. I remember one morning there was a loud bang from his room. Mum and I rushed in and found him lying on the floor unconscious.

When he came around he told us that he was lying in bed half asleep when the wall started to shimmer. He said he lay there for a while looking at it. Eventually, he decided it must be a vortex into another dimension.

Of course! That sort of thing happens all the time.

So, naturally, he tried to jump through it. It turned out not to be a vortex into another dimension at all, but merely the sun shining through the trees and in through the window and creating a shimmering effect on the wall.

I thought Mum might ban science fiction for a little while, but she didn't. Mum said, "The boy is not silly enough to throw himself headfirst at his bedroom wall twice, surely?" She was right.

Brody discovered coolness in his early teens. He found coolness and lost the power to string a series of words into a sentence. That's what being cool is, apparently, saying as little as possible. It gives one an air of mystique.

After I hang up the phone I start doing the washing-up and it occurs to me that I don't know anything about this woman who sleeps in the room next to mine.

Until now it has been as if she were blank, with no personality, except those clues given by her beautiful house.

Until this moment I haven't really thought about it as Grace's house. I know that it belongs to her, but I haven't really thought about the Grace who owns this house and the Grace I'm with every day as the same person. It has not occurred to me until this moment to wonder what she was like.

I put the dishes away and walk around the house looking for clues that would tell me more about her personality. *Who is this woman?*

I look for clues that I might have missed. I know she had expensive taste. She has beautiful things. She used to wear beautiful clothes. Her wardrobe is full of dark suits and silk blouses, but they are all new-looking, like clothes on a rack in a shop and not at all like the clothes I have been dressing her in.

When I arrived she was dressed in a tracksuit and I have been dressing her in tracksuits ever since. There is a drawer in her wardrobe full of the things. But they are not at all like the suits. Firstly, they are cheap brands. Now I'm thinking that they must have been purchased postinjury for convenience. I don't think Grace picked them out for herself.

I open the drawers in the wardrobe, looking for something old and comfortable. Didn't she have a favorite jumper or cardigan? Everybody has a favorite cardigan that they wear around the house, don't they? It might be ancient and stained and threadbare, but it's comfy. There's a clue to her personality—Grace must have thrown things out when they became old and worn. I wonder if she did that with people?

The books in the house, except in Grace's study, are leather-bound classics or glossy photography or art books. Even all the cookbooks are hardcover. None of them look read or worn in any way. Didn't she have a favorite book? A favorite recipe?

Who is Grace?

I look at the pictures in the house. There is not one picture of Grace. There are pictures on every wall in the entire house. The hallway is lined with pictures, all in a nice neat row. There are lots of stylish prints, but no personal photographs displayed. If there were photographs then I could see the expressions on her face.

The whole place looks kind of contrived, like a home furnishings catalog. It could almost be a very expensive time-share house.

How irritatingly enigmatic.

I know why I haven't thought about Grace before. There is nothing personal about this house. While everything is beautiful and meticulously displayed, there is no indication of the life of the person who lives here.

I wonder if this had been done on purpose? Everything matches. Everything is ornamental. Everything from the tassels that hold the curtains back to the brass-backed light switches. The whole house is like a stage set. It is as if Grace didn't want anyone to know anything about her but the veneer—the image that she had created for public viewing. Why is that?

I'm intrigued.

Now this—this box bursting at the seams with Grace's personality.

Before I go to bed, I sit next to Grace and watch her sleep. She lookes so peaceful and harmless and blank.

Snow White.

I wonder if she dreams?

I look closer. There are small creases around her mouth and between her eyebrows that I hadn't noticed before. So, she laughed and she frowned. I wonder if she will ever laugh and frown again?

Tomorrow morning I am going to ask the lime nightie woman next door if her house has ever been egged.

Rubber Gloves came to see me this morning. Why? Why me? I don't like her.

She said that she's had an argument with Brioney and she came over to warn me that Brioney might come over and ask to use Grace's sewing machine.

Grace sewed?

If she comes over, on no account am I to lend it to her. Charity is sick of Brioney using all her stuff. Let her go out and buy her own things.

She brought "little Jeremy" with her and he spent the whole morning chasing Prickles around and pulling his tail. Prickles jumped on the windowsill and sat there looking down at the offending child in disbelief, his long black tail swishing just out of reach.

Charity told me that Jeremy just loves animals. He's so good with animals.

Apparently Brioney was just being stupid and it's time she faced facts. Everybody knows that this man she's living with is useless. Charity was just being a caring sister. Charity only cares about what is best for Brioney. It just tears her up inside that Brioney hasn't experienced the joy of having children, and she never will if she stays with this man. Brioney's not getting any younger. A lot of older women are having children nowadays.

I look at her talking and I realize she really means it. Charity wants Brioney to have children. They fight about all sorts of things but underneath it all, Charity wants Brioney to have children. She truly believes it's a great thing and is cross with Brioney because she won't do it.

Charity tells me that she thinks it would be lovely for little Jeremy and Bianca and Simone to have a little cousin to play with. Jeremy just loves babies. He is so good with younger children.

I hope that he is better with younger children than he is with animals.

I wanted to tell her that while having kids was great for her, maybe Brioney didn't want to? Maybe it would solve a lot of problems if Charity could just get used to the idea that there are some women who just don't want to?

I thought back to what my mother had told me, about not telling people how to run their lives. Clearly Charity wasn't asking me for advice, so I just listened.

Charity has almost given up hope that her children

might have little cousins to play with. Grace was pregnant before the accident, but of course she lost the child and now she's had a hysterectomy.

"Grace was pregnant?"

"Oh, yes. We found that out in the hospital. It was in the middle of the night. I remember because I had to call the sitter. I just couldn't possibly drive myself. I was a mess. There we all were in the hospital. I didn't have any makeup on. I was all a-fluster. I didn't even have time to dab on a bit of lipstick. I must have looked a fright.

"The doctor came out and said that they were afraid she'd lost the child during the accident. We were all surprised. None of us knew. She never told a soul. Well, it's not surprising, really, being a love child. Love child sounds so much nicer than bastard, don't you think?" Charity says, patting me on the arm.

"We didn't know at the time whose it was, and I mean nobody knows for certain, but Mr. Preston's wife left him shortly before the accident so we think it must have been his." Charity shook her head and fluffed her hair out at the sides with her fingers. "And he's so protective of her and her things. He's like . . ."

"A large and growly bear," I said, thoughtfully.

I didn't realize that I'd said it out loud until Charity started chortling.

"Hoo! Hoo! A large and growly bear! That's exactly it! Brioney will love that one. . . . If I ever speak to her again."

Charity delicately scratched one eye with a long manicured fingernail. Her mouth pulled down in a really unattractive way. I thought she was upset. I thought she might even be on the verge of tears.

She's pretending not to be upset but she is. Grace didn't tell her own sister about the child—the sister for whom children are everything.

"After that we gave the doctor permission to, you know, have her done. I mean, it's much more convenient, isn't it? And she's not likely to have the opportunity again now, is she?"

Charity is cross with Grace for not telling her about the child. She can't talk to her about it, so she takes it out on Brioney.

See? I'm a psychologist now.

i went to uni this morning. As I was walking out the gate, the neighbor was leaving as well.

"Excuse me," I called out to him.

"What?" He was looking aggressive.

"Has your house ever been egged?"

"What?"

"Has your house ever been egged?" I repeated.

"What are you talking about, you dumb bitch?"

She never did it. Surely he would remember if she had.

I think quickly. "I heard that there have been some random eggings around here. That's all."

He frowned at me and turned away.

Hiro greets me as I walk down the pathway at the

university. I wonder how long the poor bloke has been hanging around the entranceway waiting for me.

I decide to try a new blush avoidance tactic. I start talking as soon as he is in hearing range and I don't stop talking until he walks away again. That way he doesn't talk and I don't have to feel embarrassed about not being able to understand him.

"Hiro!"

What if his name isn't Hiro? Oh dear, blush coming on.

"I hope you don't mind me calling you Hiro, do you? It's a term of endearment, of course."

Excellent recovery, blush is subsiding.

"So, how did it go, good? Good. Are you enjoying uni? You look like you are enjoying uni. I hope you liked my color scheme. You know, in the notes, I mean. Can't go past primary colors, I always say. Makes for happy revising, don't you think? Got to be a happy reviser. You look like a happy reviser. Are you a happy reviser? Well, you look it and that's the important thing after all, isn't it? Yellow's probably the happiest, but not so good for the eyes on a late night, I've found. You've got to look after your eyes, haven't you? Got to do all your yellow revising during the day. Anyway, it's been lovely chatting with you, Hiro, but I must fly. Ridiculous expression, of course, but it's the one they're all using. I'll be off then—busy, busy. If you need any more notes, you know where to find me. I'll be about sooner or later, as you must already know. Bye!"

Well. That went very well.

•   •   •

When I got home, I took Grace out for lunch. I have to confess that I made her walk to the main street and all the way back so she'd be tired enough to have an afternoon nap, so that I could read more from her spooky box.

So, Grace had been pregnant, apparently by Mr. Preston. So they were lovers. I wouldn't have thought it, though. When two people are intimate, when they're lovers, there's no personal space like there is with friends or relatives or acquaintances. When they touch, anywhere, it's familiar, it's even anticipated. But when Mr. Preston reaches for Grace's hand, or helps her out of her chair—or even when they danced—his touch is tentative, not familiar. There is a definite personal space between them.

We sat in this little coffee shop and watched the people walking past. I'm amused by the way people react to Grace. The waitress, thinking she was being broad-minded and tolerant, kept tucking Grace's serviette into her collar and bellowing in Grace's ear, *"Are you right, love?"* She was one of those tanned ladies with lots of gold bangles and drawn-on eyebrows.

"Are you right, love?"

Eventually I said, "Look, there's nothing wrong with her hearing."

The waitress said, "I'm just trying to help," and stormed off.

Anyway, the long walk did the trick. I brought Grace home and put her to bed.

I made myself a pint of coffee. That's my latest thing. I make coffee in a pint glass and then I don't have to get up. Although there are two drawbacks. One is that it gets sort of cold toward the end if I don't drink it fast enough. Two is that if I drink it too fast I get a bit hyper and find it difficult to concentrate.

Anyway, I'm in Grace's study with my pint of coffee and

I open up the spooky box. I pick up a piece of paper and I wander out the front and sit on the steps.

DRAFT
Alistair,

Firstly, I would like to thank you for choosing me to talk to. I have been aware of your frustration for some time. I feel honored.

Secondly, working with you I am aware of the dedication and commitment required in undertaking this job. I hope you don't find it patronizing of me to extend my heartfelt best wishes to you.

Please allow me to offer you three pieces of advice:

One: Be bold. Never miss an opportunity to let your brilliance shine and dazzle. Take that chance. Accept the challenge, or if the challenge doesn't arise, make your own challenges.

Two: Don't settle for mediocrity. Find a dream and pursue it. Allow every decision you make to bring you closer to achieving that dream.

And three: Have fun. Take time to play, because if you're not having a good tear-squirting belly laugh, chances are you're doing it wrong.

I will not wish you good luck. I don't believe luck to be a necessary ingredient for success. Instead, I wish you the wisdom to make good decisions. I'm sure you will be fabulous.

Grace

It sounds familiar. I'm sitting on the front veranda sipping a nice hot pint of coffee. Everything is a bit dry out here, so I might do a little watering.

I'm watering the front garden. Grace's tap has a little brass frog on it. Now, that's attention to detail. I'm letting my thoughts wander about. I'm going to get in there and dig out all the weeds. I've been watering the garden in the afternoons. It's already looking better.

Daisies are bobbing under the spray. There are little beads of new sprouts on the petunias. I'm waving the hose about in a big R for Rachel. All the flowers out here are pink, white or blue. Everything matches.

Grace was pregnant.

Prickles is leaning against my leg, washing himself. He looks up and winks one of his big green eyes at me.

"Don't wink at me, you saucy devil."

I rub my knuckles across his forehead. He points his ears out to the side and stalks away.

That's something else that isn't consistent. Grace is so orderly. Any pregnancy of Grace's would be meticulously planned. If she was pregnant, then why aren't there baby things around the house? Why was my bedroom made up as a guest room? There was nothing that would indicate that she was expecting a child.

Now it's coming back to me. I've heard Grace's words before. In my head I can see Mr. Preston standing there, see the words coming out of his mouth.

It was the same thing word for word. I couldn't believe it. I remember being so impressed when I heard it at my graduation. Anything can be "easy-peasy" if you're just regurgitating someone else's words. I felt cheated. I felt that Grace had been cheated. They were her sentiments and he took them as his own.

I remember everyone clapping for him. I remember him shaking his head so modestly. He had made it sound so spontaneous. How can this be? I remember him talking about her and her "life" so passionately.

I turn off the hose and wind it back up in a neat pile.

I take a big swig of coffee. It's cold. *Bleagh, bleagh.*

I wander back inside and I sit down in the bedroom where Grace is sleeping. She has such soft, pale skin, almost translucent. I can see the blueness of her veins in her neck and forehead. I can see the very fine downy hair across her face, her cheek and jawbone. She is very beautiful, in a handsome way, not in a "pretty" way.

"Can you hear me?" I ask her quietly. "Do you know what's going on? Are you in there?"

She opens her eyes and *looks* at me. They were shut and now they are wide open looking at me. Just for a moment I think I see something behind her eyes. Just for a moment.

I stand up suddenly. My heart is beating really fast. Her eyes follow me.

As I stand up, I spill some cold coffee on my shoe. I look down.

When I look back at Grace, her eyes are closed again.

I stand and look at her for another minute. My heart is beating really hard. "Shit," I say out aloud. Freaky. That was so freaky.

I tiptoe into the study, watching Grace's face as I walk around the bed. Her eyes stay closed.

I put the note back in the spooky box, pick up the next piece of paper and read.

Things I didn't say in my farewell speech
Andre, you little Hitler, thank you for teaching me every-thing anyone ever wanted to know about how not to be a manager.

You run your department like a prison camp. You quash any hint of creativity, any tiny spark of inspiration that any of your downtrodden and oppressed staff dare to demonstrate.

I imagine that you must have very small genitals. I hope to God that I have never been an unconscious partic-ipant in any of your unwholesome thoughts.

You are a weasel. Worse, you are a weasel that even other weasels shy away from.

Dimitre, you are so lazy that you couldn't even muster the energy to steal my ideas. You are cowardly, weak and stupid. You are so visibly incompetent that I haven't even bothered to point out your inadequacies. I am astounded that you have the decisiveness to dress yourself every day.

I look forward to not having to compensate for both of your profound inabilities.

My final words to each of you are as follows:

Andre, I hope the staff in your department prepare a violent and shocking revolution, and that your career prospects are torn forcibly into gory, unsalvageable pieces.

Dimitre, you have to wake up each morning and go to bed every night being who you are. I don't need to wish any further curses on you.

Mr. Preston came to see Grace in the evening but I'd called the nurse so I could get in a little revision and maybe read ahead a bit. Jan was taking Grace out for a walk.

Jan still calls me "darl." It must be much easier than remembering people's names. I might find a generic nickname with which I shall address all—"turtledove," for example, or is that too intimate? Perhaps "cohort."

When he found Grace wasn't at home, Mr. Preston was going to leave, but I asked him to have a cup of coffee with me. I switched on the jug and took two cups out of the cupboard. Grace has these funky stainless steel cups and saucers. I just love them. I wanted him to tell me more about Grace. She sounded like a complete bitch—but with excellent dress sense. I liked her.

"Come sit by me a while, cohort," I said.

"I'm sorry?" he asked, perplexed.

"I'm trying out some generic means by which to address people," I explained, "like Jan does."

"Oh, of course," he replied, sitting by me. "What about chum?"

I considered for a moment. "Chum is good. May I call you chum?"

"Certainly."

We sat quietly for a while, sipping coffee.

"What was she like? Was she nice?" I asked him.

He laughed. "No. She's not nice. She's lots of things but she's not *nice*. She attacked everyone," he said, reaching for the coffee plunger. "Grace started out as a secretary, a personal assistant I guess you would call it today. She was very good—efficient. She worked for a friend of mine before she came to work for us. She's always worked in law or finance. This guy was an accountant."

So they worked together.

I fill my funky coffee cup with a little milk.

Mr. Preston leans back, crossing one ankle over the other. "He used to complain about her, this friend of mine. He thought she was too frank. Of course that's not the way he put it. We would be having a drink or playing a round of golf and he would tell us stories about her. He gave her the sack eventually. Apparently she wasn't working out "personality-wise." She was impudent and difficult and she refused to make coffee. She was particularly obstinate about not making coffee. She wouldn't make coffee when she first came to work with me, either."

So she worked *for* him. He was her boss.

Mr. Preston pours the coffee and spoons in some sugar. "The story goes that there were two guys who used to complain about her a lot. They were young accountants. They were the department heads or whatever. Everyone complained at some stage, but those two in particular. I think they were Italian, or was it Greek?" He shrugged. "They were Mediterranean, anyway. Grace gave them hell. She wouldn't cover for them. Eventually they got her sacked. Apparently those two guys sang 'Ding Dong, the Witch Is Dead' at her farewell dinner. Subtle."

Andre and Dimitre?

Prickles wanders over and jumps up on Mr. Preston's lap. He rubs his knuckles across the cat's head absently. Prickles closes his eyes, smiling and purring.

Cantankerous cat.

Mr. Preston takes a sip of his coffee. "She looked for work for a while after that. We sent her to see other people that we knew. We didn't have any positions open at the time. But, well . . ."

Who's "we"?

"Everyone knew that she was good, but she was too outspoken. Frankness was a crime punishable by death for a secretary in those days. It probably still is, to be honest."

I take a sip of my coffee. I make the *ooosh too hot* sound, close associate of *ooosh paper cut*. Accompanied by a small frown, *ooosh* indicates small injury in any culture across the globe. It's universal, like laughter. No use for large injuries, though. Nobody says *ooosh lost an arm*, or *ooosh bullet penetrating large muscle group*.

Mr. Preston is patting Prickles on the head, not stroking, *patting*, and Prickles is kneading his little paws like mad with his little tongue poking out. I can't believe this! Grace should have called him Fickle.

"She eventually got a job with one of the golf buddies. She told me that at the interview he asked her if she got on with her previous employers and she said that she did. A couple of weeks later he put his hand up her skirt. When she objected, he said, 'But you said at the interview that you "got on" with your bosses.' She resigned, she made a real fuss, but it was all buried."

Mr. Preston takes another slurp of his coffee.

"We didn't play golf together anymore. It was after that I gave her a job. One of our ladies had gone off on maternity leave."

Mr. Preston pushes Prickles off his lap and wipes the cat hair off his trousers. Does Prickles stalk off in a huff? No. He lifts a little paw, batting Mr. Preston on the leg like Oliver. *Please, sir, can I have some more?*

Mr. Preston is gently pushing the cat away. Prickles is rubbing his face against Mr. Preston's hand affectionately, arching his back and turning around in circles.

"She wasn't nice, but she didn't have it easy. She was a single woman out on her own. No matter what you might hear about equal opportunity, there is still a mindset. You've got to remember that only thirty years ago single women couldn't even get loans from the bank. They were supposed to be married or at home waiting to get married."

Mr. Preston looked at me and smiled. "Grace was part of the generation that brought about the changes in attitude you enjoy today."

Here we go: "The feminist movement part one"—guest speaker, middle-aged, middle-class, Anglo-Saxon man. Yeah, right.

Mr. Preston bent down and picked up Prickles, who had been winding himself around his ankles. "Grace was never what you would describe as nice, but she was an ambitious, intelligent woman. She went to university at night and studied law. She wanted to be a partner. Ambitious and intelligent women can be scary for men, even today. At least today they have a slim chance of recognition. Grace was never going to get that. She was bitter about never being given the opportunity."

In spades.

"Did you give her recognition when she worked for you?" I challenged.

Mr. Preston frowned. "It was never my decision." He scratched the cat under the chin and put him down on the ground again.

"We were the leading organization at that time. We still are. My family has always lived here. My great-grandfather looked after the great-grandfathers of clients I have today. When Grace came, she got to know all the clients. She took good care of them, even the difficult ones. I was always aware of the important role Grace played in our organization. She was very good. She knew the law. She knew her job, but she wanted to do more.

"We always looked after our staff. Grace had pay raise after pay raise, but she didn't want more money, she wanted to do more. She wanted to practice law. She thought it was her right. It probably was, but it just wasn't *done*. My father always said that the clients wouldn't accept her. He said she lacked experience. Besides, she was good at her job, really good. We didn't want to have to replace her, so we gave her more money—the sort of money she wouldn't get anywhere else. If she wanted to practice somewhere else, she would have had to start at the bottom again."

"You must have spent a lot of time with her here," I said, probing.

"Yes." Mr. Preston looked me directly in the eye.

How're you off for socks and jocks?

I could feel a blush coming on. I picked up his cup and took it into the kitchen.

That's all I was going to get for today.

After Mr. Preston left, I washed the dishes. I had been going to do a little revision but I found myself wandering back into Grace's study. I took the spooky box out from behind the books, opened the lid and read.

● ● ●

> *The evening star doesn't rise so much as it appears.*
> *I am watching and waiting for the evening star to appear.*
> *The clouds are glowing gold on the edge of the sky. Soon they will fade away into darkness.*
> *I went to see that man you sent me to today.*
> *I thrust out my chin and dared him to "interview" me. He sat rubbing his jaw and observing me like fauna. Like game. I didn't know whether he was going to ask me my typing speed or my fellatio technique.*
> *So I asked him.*

Why do they do this? Why do these men sit with legs splayed, exhibiting themselves? I have nothing against raw sexuality, but I do believe there is a time and a place for it.

Where does this unconscious disdain come from? These coffee-making expectations?

What I wouldn't give for a penis during this period of job-searching.

There it is. The only star in the sky. Darkness enfolds the once gilt-edged clouds.

Why are you putting me through this?

I made a pile of the pieces of paper that I had read so far. Then I found a piece of gold ribbon in the box. I wondered if the ribbon, like Kate's train ticket, was some keepsake—some memento of a special time, some part of Grace's life that was important to her, its significance lost now forever.

I sat at the desk and wrapped the gold ribbon around my index finger, feeling its rough texture on the pad of my thumb. How did she come to possess this little piece of gold ribbon?

I tied it around the pieces of paper that I had read so far.

I reached into the box again and pulled out a black-and-white studio photograph scalloped at the edges. It showed three little girls, smiling coyly. The biggest girl had a baby on her lap and she was holding the baby's hands in her own. They all had short curly hair. Their cheeks had been painted pink, their eyes blue, and the folds of their short puffed sleeves had been outlined with white crayon so they glimmered.

This must be Charity, Brioney and Angelica. This baby must be Grace. I brought the photo right up to my face and looked at it.

I don't know how long I sat there with that photograph under my nose. It was as if I were in a trance. I studied every part of her face, trying to find some similarity between this infant and the woman I care for. I could see that it was her, but I don't know how.

I tucked the photo in under the ribbon.

I pulled out the next piece of paper, leant back in the chair and read.

For A. Preston

Enclosed are copies of the relevant correspondence and documents re: client number 0829 for your perusal.

Client's name is Eleanor Samerchi (pronounced "samhersh"). NOTE: POTENTIAL DISASTER IMMINENT.

An appointment has been made for you at 9:25, expect her at 9:10.

She will be accompanied by her father, Athol Porter, whom you will remember from your first briefing in September. Mr. Samerchi is away on business overseas and will be back on Tuesday.

Ms. Samerchi has written a fairly extensive novel on her grievances. (Please find attached.) I have underlined the relevant sections and summarized the five most important points (please observe notes in red, which are suggested responses). If she doesn't swallow those, revert to clause twelve in her contract. Bless whoever wrote clause twelve.

You have a fictitious appointment at 10:15, which
you may graciously choose to break, or use if you need to
withdraw and regroup. (Please use the usual signal.)
I will be home from 7:00 p.m. if you need to phone.
May the force be with you.
Grace

As I tucked the memo under the ribbon and put all the things I had read back in the box, I wondered why she had kept it.

I walked back into the lounge room to check on Grace. "How would you like a bath?" I said to her.

While I ran a bath for Grace, I opened the bathroom cabinet. It is filled with lotions and creams and bottles and little pots. I work my way along the shelves, turning them around so I can see the labels. There are exfoliating scrubs, mud masks, peeling masks, moisturizers, scented oils, day creams, night creams and bubble baths.

Hmm, is someone a little neurotic about aging, then?

I pull out a whole bunch of bottles I find in there and put them into the basin.

I put some jasmine-scented bath oil in the bathwater, walk back into the living room and open the CD cupboard. I put on Chopin and pull Grace up from the chair. I lead her into the bathroom and take her clothes off and put her in the bath. I sit on the edge of the bath and smear a mud mask on her face. I fold up a hand towel and place it behind her head.

Grace lies there underneath the bubbles, looking straight ahead.

"Are you enjoying yourself, turtledove?"

Grace doesn't answer.

I stand up and smear the mud mask on my own face. I turn the taps off and walk back into the living room, leaving the bathroom door open.

I walk into the study and pick up the spooky box. I bring it into the lounge room and place it on the coffee table.

I take out a postcard. There is a picture of a dolphin jumping out of a pool to catch a piece of fish that a man is holding. Words stamped in gold foil at the bottom of the card say, "Greetings from Coffs Harbor."

I turn the card over. It is addressed to Grace. The hand is old-fashioned, with flourishes and loops on the g's and f's.

> *Hello my love,*
> *We are having a wonderful time up here. Your father has almost made himself sick eating chocolate-coated bananas, like always.*
> *I'm looking forward to seeing Aunty Ida tomorrow. We're going to stop with her for a spell. I'll give her your love.*
> *We had dinner in your favorite seafood restaurant last night, the one near the marina.*
> *I know it's corny to say so on a postcard, but I do wish you'd decided to come with us this year, Gracey. A holiday would do you good. It would keep your mind off things.*
> *All my love,*
> *Mum*

I sat there looking at the postcard, turning it over in my hands.

When my mask was dry I put the postcard back in the box and put the box back in the study.

I went into the bathroom and washed the mud mask off my face. I washed Grace's hair and face. I used a big sponge, squeezing the water out over her head. I helped her out of the bath and wrapped her in a big fluffy bathrobe. I sat her on top of the toilet and rubbed some night cream into her face and neck, and then rubbed some moisturizing cream into my own face.

"There, now we are beautiful!" I said to Grace.

I pulled on her jammy jams and put her to bed. I sat up next to her and read aloud for a while. Prickles jumped onto the bed and curled up in the crook of Grace's knees.

Grace's face was shiny in the light of the bedside lamp.

When Grace was asleep, I walked around the house turning off lights and locking the doors. I hopped into my own bed. I lay there for a while on my back, resting my head on my forearm.

I thought about the postcard from Grace's mother. It was an ordinary postcard, saying all the normal things that people say on postcards.

I started to drift off. There's nothing like a bit of pampering to give you a good, long, relaxing sleep.

I took Grace to the movies this morning. There
is one of those huge cinema complexes in the shopping center about ten minutes away. Grace's house is so central! If
nothing else, this girl has an eye for real estate.

I dressed her up, put makeup on her face and even
blow-dried her hair with a big round brush. I didn't dress
her in a tracksuit. I found a long burgundy dress in the
wardrobe and put her new shoes on her feet. She looked
pretty good.

I took her in the car. Luckily the theater isn't too far away,
because I only have the one snorkel. Before I left I got a piece
of paper and I rolled it into a cone shape and put it in Grace's

mouth. I curled her hand into a fist around it, but she wasn't having a bit of it. I put the snorkel in the glove box.

When I was buying the tickets, Grace was standing at the edge of the entrance area, looking out at the pinball parlor across the corridor. She was standing there on the ugly carpet they always have in the foyer at cinemas.

While I was standing in line, I kept turning around to check on her. She just looked like a normal person lost in thought. People were bustling about around her and she just stood there with her arms by her sides. That's sort of what she is like—someone who is lost in thought all the time.

I'm being served. I poke my money through the little hole in the glass at the counter. As I turn around, shoving the change into my purse, I can see a teenage boy, probably about fifteen, walking toward Grace. He's about as far away from her as I am, coming from the opposite direction. I can see the aggression in the way he is moving. His chest is puffed out and his face is really hostile.

"What are you staring at?" he yells at her from five meters and closing. I walk toward Grace, fast.

"I'm talking to you." He's pointing at her. I can see the muscles in his shoulders and arms tense. "What are you staring at?"

I reach her and grab her by the shoulders. The boy stands still when he sees that she is not alone.

As I turn her around, the boy is backing away. "You dumb slut!" he yells over his shoulder as he disappears back into the pinball parlor.

"Well, that was unpleasant, wasn't it?" I say to Grace as we walk away. I'm trying to keep calmness in my voice, but I'm shaken.

I'm wondering what brought that on? I wonder what would have happened if I hadn't been there. Would he have hit her?

What was his problem? I think it must be some kind of prehistoric pack mentality surging through in the hormones, the same kind of survival of the fittest thing that I observed so often in the schoolyard.

Weak person! Weak person! Attack! Attack!

I can feel my blood pulsing through my veins. I'm trying to relax.

I hand in our tickets and we take a seat in the middle of the theater.

We watch the latest animated offering. Not exactly highbrow. I have always taken my brother to see those movies to disguise my desire to see them, but he's a bit old for that now. He's too cool. He doesn't mind coming to see the computer-generated animations—purely for academic reasons, of course.

Grace has provided me with a new excuse.

I love those movies. I love cartoons. I love how the lead character just breaks into song and they all do a little dance and everyone knows the steps, knows the chorus. I love the fact that in these movies everyone *can* sing. Wouldn't the world be a wonderful place if everybody could sing?

Just once, I would like to be in a shopping center, or waiting in a queue or some other ordinary situation, and have someone start singing and have everyone join in and start tap-dancing. There is definitely not enough spontaneous tap dancing these days.

•   •   •

We drove home again, and I changed Grace into a tracksuit and sat her out on the front veranda in one of the big comfy chairs.

I walked into her bedroom and opened the long cream curtains. Then I sat in the study with my back to the desk, looking through the wardrobe and through the bedroom window to where Grace was sitting. I lifted the lid off the spooky box and read.

I was so angry. I was driving home and I was filled with rage.

How dare you!

I was driving like a lunatic. Might have nearly killed several other people and myself.

How dare you!

You do this to me all the time. It makes me so angry. I can feel my anger rising up inside me and I can feel my heart beating. Do I say anything? No. You never give me the opportunity. Why bother giving me the authority to make decisions? You waltz into the meeting and override all the decisions I have made.

It has taken me weeks and weeks of work to put those systems into place. You didn't even have the courtesy to discuss this with me.

The decision I made on the Pritchard file was based on hours of negotiation and common sense, not to mention profitability.

How dare you humiliate me and undermine me so publicly! You make me look like a fool. I hate it when you do that. The money that we will lose! I could have slapped you.

But of course, I didn't.

I pull up the car with a jolt. Keys won't come out of the ignition. Everything falls out of my handbag. Freezing cold. House will be like an iceberg. It's so late. I had to stay back and reverse all the paperwork. So much for being efficient. I get out of the car. You were sitting on the doorstep. "Get out of my face, you bastard."

You had this big black overcoat on with the collar turned up. Your lips are blue. You are standing between the door and me. You say nothing. Then you take something out of your pocket. I can't see what it is. It is so dark and it blends in with the black leather gloves you are wearing.

It squeaks. You hold it up to my face. Your blue lips smiling.

It is a tiny black kitten, with a little gold ribbon around its neck. It shivers. "Meow." Big eyes. Big green eyes. Little pink tongue. Little meow.

"I don't know what you want to call him, but I've been calling him Pritchard."

I hate it when you do this. I'm torn with indecision. I long to fold myself inside your overcoat, where it is warm and safe.

I looked up. Grace was gone. I could hear an awful screeching noise, like cats fighting, and laughter—nasty laughter.

I threw the paper back into the box and ran out to the veranda. Grace was standing at the end of the veranda with her hands on the railing, swaying from foot to foot.

The laughter was coming from the lime nightie woman

next door, although she wasn't in the lime nightie now. She was standing on her veranda. She was doubled over, holding her belly, laughing. Shouter had Prickles. He was standing in the middle of the lawn facing Grace. He had Prickles and was throwing him in the air above his head and catching him by the stomach. He's sneering, "Hey, Nuffy. I gotcher caaat." *Heave*.

Prickles flies up into the air and lets out a long screech. His fur is all standing up. Screamer is laughing uncontrollably. Prickles is writhing in the air, turning himself around in the air. Shouter catches Prickles on the way down again.

"Hey, Nuffy, I gotcher caaat."

I run out on the veranda. I bellow, "Put the cat down!"

When I get angry I bellow, not a high squeak like a lot of people but a deep bellow from way down in the bottom of my guts. I take a deep breath and it comes out loud and low like a foghorn.

Prickles is on the way up again, but Shouter doesn't try to catch him this time, he looks at me, still sneering. He pulls his foot back and watches the cat writhing in the air before him, aims and lays a boot into the cat at about waist height.

When the boot hits him, Prickles' legs wrap around Shouter's foot for a moment and then he rebounds off. He moans as he sails through the air and falls in a heap on our front lawn. He rolls over slowly and lets out a long wail.

I'm running down the steps. I'm running across the lawn. I can hear the screen door shut behind them as they go back into the house, but I'm looking at Prickles. He isn't moving.

Grace is standing on the veranda. She is swaying rapidly

from foot to foot. She has her hands up to her temples and she's making a short breathy sound, "Eeeh, eeeh, eeh."

I run over to where Prickles is lying on the lawn. His tail flicks once. Tears are running down my cheeks. He looks up at me groggily and then his little green eyes close.

Oh, no, oh, no, oh, no.

I'm grunting. I'm kneeling down on the ground over the cat.

Oh no, oh no, what do I do, what do I do.

I can't see because I've got hot, angry tears spilling out of my eyes. I'm blinking furiously. My hot tears are dropping onto his black fur. I brush them off.

He's not moving, he's not moving, oh no, No, NO!

I get up and run inside. I grab my car keys from off the kitchen bench and a towel from the bathroom.

Back on the lawn. Kneeling. Prickles is lying very still, his eyes closed.

OH NO, OH NO, OH NO!

I pick him up gently. He is limp in my hands. His head is hanging down over my wrist. I put him on the towel and I wrap him up. I carry him to my car. His head is hanging down out of the towel.

I lay him down on the backseat. He's lying on a funny angle.

Oh no, oh no, oh no.

I run back up the stairs and put my arm around Grace's waist. I lead her down the stairs. Her hands are still up in the air and her elbow hits me right in the bridge of the nose. Pain shoots up behind my eyes, and for a moment I can't see.

"It's OK, turtledove, take it easy," I say, trying to sound

calm, but my voice is all scratchy, as if someone has poured a bucket of sand down my throat.

I push her into the car.

I run around the car. I bang my knee on the bumper. I jump in the car.

Please be alive, please be alive.

I start the car and roar off down the street. I can't see where I'm going because there are tears in my eyes, and I'm seeing stars. Grace is twisted around, leaning into the backseat.

Hurry, hurry, hurry.

I pull up at the curb outside the vet's, four blocks away. I lift Prickles up and put him in the curve of my forearm. He's so small and limp.

I open the door of the passenger side. I pull Grace out with my free arm, not bothering to close the door behind me; we rush into the surgery.

The woman at the desk smiles as I walk in. There is a man with a birdcage on his knee and an old woman with a sleepy Alsatian lying at her feet.

"Kicked."

It's all I can say. I'm wiping my sleeve across my eyes. I feel as though I've got a grapefruit wedged in my throat.

"Kicked," I say to the woman. Tears are pouring out of my eyes. Grace is swaying next to me with her arms folded across her chest.

I'm holding out the towel bundle in my hands, stretched out toward the lady behind the desk.

"Kicked. In here."

The woman frowns at me but does not speak. She stands up and opens a door behind her desk.

A moment later the vet comes out. He's about thirty, with dark hair. As he moves around the desk I can see jeans under his white coat.

"I'm sorry," he says to the birdcage man and the Alsatian woman, "do you mind, if I see this little . . ." He lifts the edge of the towel in my arm and peeks in, ". . . fellow?" They shake their heads in unison, and the vet ushers me through the doorway.

I put Prickles down on the stainless steel table and unwrap the towel.

"Now," says the vet, "this is?" I look at him.

A cat.

I'm not saying anything. No words are coming out.

A cat, a cat, you're the vet here, you're supposed to be the expert in this scenario. A cat, a kicked cat.

"Prickles." Fresh tears spill out of the corners of my eyes.

"And you say he's been kicked, is that right?" The vet is pulling up Prickles' eyelids and gently feeling each of his legs.

"Very hard. Very hard." I can't breathe. My mouth is full of saliva and tears.

The vet looks at Grace. "I think we have met Prickles before, yes?"

"She doesn't speak," I say, wiping my eyes with my sleeve again.

"English?" he asks.

"No, she just doesn't speak."

I wasn't doing a very good job of speaking either.

The vet nods, he's feeling Prickles' belly. "I would like to take a look in here, I think."

"He's alive?" I whispered. Fresh tears spring, actually spring. They're splashing on the stainless steel bench.

"Oh, yes"—the vet smiles at me—"but we have at least two broken ribs and I would really like to take a little look inside."

The woman from the front desk comes through the door. The vet turns to her. "Ah, Marie, we're just going to have a little peek inside Prickles here, could you . . . please?"

Marie nods and leads us back out through the foyer. "Has Prickles been here before?" she asks as she opens the filing cabinet next to her desk and flicks through the files. She pulls out a little blue card. "Ahh yes, here we go, look at that, vaccinations regular as clockwork, desexing at six months. Abscess drained two years ago. You're a very responsible pet owner, Grace."

"I'm Rachel. This is Grace."

Marie smiles at us both. "Is this the contact number?" She hands me the blue card.

"Yes."

"Now, you go home. Make yourself a nice cup of tea. We'll ring you up in a little while and tell you how Prickles is doing, OK?"

I lead Grace back out to the car, which looks like an abandoned getaway vehicle, parked askew with three doors open.

When we get home, the front door is open. I take Grace inside and sit her in her chair. I flick on the jug and pick up the telephone.

"Mr. Preston, it's Rachel," I say in a terribly dramatic on-the-verge-of-tears voice.

"What's happened? Is Grace OK?" he said.

"It's Pritchard."

Oops. That's a slipup.

"Who?"

"Prickles."

"What's happened."

"Shouter," I begin.

Oops, and another.

"I mean the man next door, he drop-kicked him about three meters. He's at the vet."

Silence. I thought for a moment that maybe I'd lost the connection.

"I'll be right over."

Mr. Preston arrived about fifteen minutes later. I'm having a nice cup of tea as instructed. I'm sitting on the couch taking big hiccuppy breaths and making little whimpering noises.

"What's going on?" He strides in, shrugging out of his big navy jacket and then rolling up his shirtsleeves.

"The guy from next door." I start to speak and begin to cry again.

Mr. Preston sits down on the couch and points with his thumb over his shoulder toward Shouter and Screamer's house. "This bloke?"

"Yes, he had a hold of Prickles and he threw him in the air a couple of times and then booted him in the guts."

"You saw this from where?"

"I was inside. I could hear the cat screaming, so I ran out on the veranda just before he kicked him."

"And then you did what?"

"I ran over to the cat and picked him up and took him to the vet with Grace and he's being operated on now. The vet says he has broken ribs."

"That's it?" He pulls his mobile phone out of his pocket.

I nod. "Except Grace was watching what was going on and she was reacting."

"What did she do?" he says, fixing me with a piercing stare.

"She was swaying and holding her head and making a noise," I reply.

Mr. Preston punches a number into his mobile and sits back on the couch with one long arm across the top.

"Ben . . . Ben, I know you're there, Ben."

I'm wondering why Mr. Preston knows Shouter's phone number.

"Don't give me crap, you know exactly who I am. I am the man who's going to take you out to the course and beat the crap out of you, and you know I can. I've done it before and I'll do it again."

I can hear the squeak of a voice on the other end of the line.

"No, pal, you listen, you just don't get it, do you? I'll explain it to you again. You hold on to the leather end and you hit the ball with the metal end."

I'm lost now.

Mr. Preston listens for a moment and then he tilts his head and smiles. "No, seriously, Ben, we've got a little problem over here, a man has just kicked the cat of a friend of mine, on purpose. He's picked it up and drop-kicked it about three meters. The cat's at the vet. We don't know if the little bloke is going to make it."

Mr. Preston is quiet for a moment; then he says the address, looking over at me. "Is he in there now?" he asks, pointing his thumb over his shoulder again.

"I think so," I say.

"We're pretty sure the bloke's at home. Yeah, he lives next door, mate. On the right as you're coming up the street."

I can hear the squeak of the voice at the other end of the line. Mr. Preston is smiling. "You know I love you like a brother, Ben. No worries, I'll see you soon."

Mr. Preston puts his phone back in his pocket. "Now, you say Grace was reacting."

I tell him about what Grace was doing, and he makes me get up and do a demonstration. Then we go out on the veranda and I show him what happened.

"Well, now we might just sit ourselves out here and see what happens," he says, rubbing his hands together. He brings Grace outside and sits her down in one of the big comfy chairs. Mr. Preston leans against the railing facing us. I can hear sirens approaching—sirens, plural.

Mr. Preston grins. "That'll be Ben." He looks at his watch. "That was quick."

Two police cars race up the street, sirens blaring, and pull up in front of the house next door. Three police officers jump out of the cars, two of them walk up to the neighbors' door, pulling their hats on. The other, a middle-aged man with gray hair, saunters over and leans on the picket fence.

"I'm here to arrest you for fraudulently claiming to be a golfer, A.P. Now are you going to confess, or am I going to have to take you back to the scene of the crime?"

"You'll never take me alive, Officer," says Mr. Preston. He steps off the veranda and shakes the policeman's hand warmly. "Benjamin, how're Fran and the kids?"

"Well," says the policeman, taking his hat off and scratching his head. "Jessica's going to have a baby." He grins.

Mr. Preston says, "A grandpa again, hey? Well, that's wonderful news." He turns back toward the veranda. "These are my friends Rachel and Grace."

"Good morning," says Ben the police officer, smiling at me.

The screen door opens and Shouter, handcuffed, comes out meekly between the two police officers. They push him in the back of the police car.

"Cuffs, Benjamin?" says Mr. Preston.

"Well, I'm of the belief that it's not such a big leap from kicking cats to assaulting people, and I have the safety of my officers to consider," Benjamin says, smiling at us. The smile fades. "No, seriously, mate, this is the kind of stuff I hate. It makes me angry, and I'm not the kind of bloke that gets angry. It's not for money, it's not provoked, it's just cruel. We like to bring them up with a jolt, you know? Might save us some trouble later on."

One of the police officers saunters over to us. Benjamin says to him, "You might like to take some details from these young ladies about what happened here today."

The police officer nods and takes a notebook out of his pocket. I tell him what happened and he writes it all down. I show him the exact spot where Shouter was standing, where Prickles landed and where Grace and I were standing.

Mr. Preston and Benjamin have wandered off down the street and are chatting to each other, smiling and laughing.

The two police officers take Shouter away. Benjamin and Mr. Preston shake hands again. Benjamin sits in his police car and winds down the window. "Nice to meet you, ladies." He turns to Mr. Preston, grinning. "You know that I love you like a brother."

He starts the car and drives away.

Mr. Preston stands with his hands on his hips and watches the car driving up the street. He turns back to me. "Well, now that's taken care of, I'd better go." He opens the car door and climbs in. The passenger side window glides down. "Give me a call when you hear from the vet. See you, chum," he says to me through the window, and then drives away.

I take Grace back inside.

The phone rings. It's Marie from the vet's. She tells me that Prickles is going to make it, but he's badly bruised and will be sore for a while. I can pick him up in about three days.

Kate rang this evening. She says that she's having some friends over and would I like to come. I look at Grace sitting in her chair.

No Prickles.

I tell her that I will come over if I can get someone to mind Grace.

I don't want to call the nurse. What I really want is for Mr. Preston to come over, because he would be sensitive about Grace missing her cat.

I ring him to tell him that the cat's OK and ask if he will mind Grace. He says that he will be over at seven.

As I hang up the phone I feel bad about going out after the day Grace has had. Maybe I should ring back and say that

I will stay? No, the damage is done. Mr. Preston already knows that I was prepared to go out and leave her. I don't know why, but it's important for him to think well of me.

I put Grace into her jammy jams, sit her on the lounge and put the telly on. She's not watching it.

I'm getting dressed. What does one wear to these kinds of things?

When I was at school there used to be parties. I went to one. It was held at the house of someone I didn't know. I drank too much and spent the whole night throwing up. The first time I missed and got the stupid apricot rug thing on the top of the toilet.

Who has those? Why do they have those? What possible purpose do they serve? Who sits on the top of the toilet lid? Who spends so much time sitting on top of the toilet lid that they need a little apricot rug?

One of my friends kept coming into the toilet, pulling my hair back and saying "Are you right, mate?" It was the most humiliating experience. The following Monday at school, the girl who held the party ran around and told everyone about me being sick on her stupid little apricot rug, and how slack it was because I didn't even know her. So presumably it's OK to be sick on someone's little apricot rug if you *know* them?

All the other students teased me about it relentlessly. I never went to another party. As a result, I don't know what you are supposed to wear.

I pull on a pair of jeans and boots that look like work boots.

I spend an hour trying to make my hair look as if I haven't done anything to it. It ends up looking as if I haven't done anything to it, but not in a cool, casual way, more in a just-woke-up-from-a-very-bad-dream way. I give up.

I find a little white tailored shirt with a gray pinstripe in Grace's wardrobe and I put it on, rolling up the sleeves.

I put on some red lipstick that will blend nicely with my blushes.

I sit next to Grace on the couch, put my arm around her and give her a little hug. She's still not watching telly.

Mr. Preston arrives. He's not wearing a suit. Instead he has on the standard uniform of suits that aren't wearing a suit—a navy polo shirt with mustard trousers, brown shoes and a matching belt.

Mr. Preston wears the shiniest shoes.

My mother says you can tell a lot about a person's lifestyle choice from their shoes. She says the shinier and newer a person's shoes are, the more choice they have.

He comes in with a stack of these little wee pizza boxes with the holes in the sides. I can smell them and my mouth starts to water. I love Turkish pizza.

"I like your shirt," he says as he makes his way down the hallway. "Will you have some pizza before you go?"

Oh, all right then.

Mr. Preston opens the boxes. He squeezes some lemon juice on the pizzas.

Mmmm, Turkish pizza.

He puts a long strip of pizza in Grace's hand and she eats it.

"What's this rubbish you're watching?" Mr. Preston asks. He's poking pieces of pizza down his neck—whole. I'm about to defend myself but I look up and I see that it is indeed rubbish.

Mr. Preston picks up the remote and starts flicking.

Flick, flick, flick.

The news. I figure he'll be distracted and won't notice how much of his pizza I'm eating.

How come, if someone offers you something they're eating suddenly it's the most delicious thing you've ever tasted? Salt and vinegar chips are the worst. If someone offers one a salt and vinegar chip one always eats it very slowly, thinking *This is the best chip I have ever had in my whole life.* One is always too polite to ask for another, but thinks instead, *As soon as I'm out of view, I'm buying myself a bag of salt and vinegar chips.*

"See you, chum," I say.

"Have a good time, chum," he replies.

Inside the car, I pop in the snorkel, wishing I hadn't put on the red lipstick, which is now all over my chin and my nose. It's one of those stay-on-forever lipsticks. It doesn't stay on the lips, but get it on the chin and nose and you can bet it'll be there all night.

The evening is mild. I drive along the streets with my snorkel out the window. There are couples walking their dogs and fit people in short shorts jogging. There are people dressed up for dinner walking toward the restaurant strip. I drive past the park. There are people unpacking barbecues. They have their picnic baskets and their Eskies.

Kate lives in a long street of terrace houses. The renovated ones have terra-cotta pavers with matching terra-cotta pots on their verandas, and gloss-painted wrought-iron filigree fences in emerald or maroon. They have timber venetian blinds on their timber French doors.

The unrenovated ones have rusty wrought-iron filigree

fences and cemented front lawns. They have aluminum windows covered by thick white venetian blinds.

There are all sorts of cars parked up on the footpath, from Jaguars and BMWs to Combis and Datos.

Maxwell opens the door for me, then goes outside to wait on the veranda.

What is he waiting for? He's here! This is it, isn't it?

Inside, Kate is perched on her favorite velvet cushion. She's holding a little white flower. She looks so much like a fairy in a little green floral dress that I'm about to ask her if I was supposed to come in fancy dress. I get as far as "Was I . . ." before I realize that it isn't fancy dress, it's a funky outfit, but I'm close enough to saying it to muster a nice big red blush.

"You're early, have you been running?" she asks.

I say yes, because it's easier than explaining that I'm blushing because I thought her funky outfit was a fancy-dress costume.

Maxwell is standing in the doorway looking up and down the street, rising up and down on the balls of his feet, waiting, waiting. He's wearing black leather pants and his shoes squeak.

"Maxwell, darling, can you put some music on?" Kate asks.

Maxwell turns around. "What?"

"I said, could you please put some music on."

If she has to say everything twice tonight I'm going to have to kill him. It's unbearable, it's a form of torture. It's a bit like sentence-finishers. I always want to say something really unexpected just to throw them off. I can never think quickly enough, though.

Kate and I talk about uni. She asks me if I've been to the bar. I decide that I should ask Hiro to come and see a band with me. If there is a band playing we won't have to speak and I won't have an opportunity to get embarrassed.

We chat about people at the café. I ask after the chef, the other waiters and the regulars.

Then we make poo jokes and laugh hysterically. As a general rule I am not a big fan of the poo joke, but Kate is a funny girl and she has me rolling about on my big velvet cushion. Maxwell is standing in the doorway looking disapproving.

At about nine-thirty when I'm ready to go to bed (being a morning person), people start arriving. All of a sudden the house is packed to capacity. I'm introduced to about fifteen people; they were all born in the early 1970s so they have names like Vladimir and Paris.

I'm sharing my big velvet cushion with a girl called Charisma, which is unfortunate really, but her parents weren't to know at the time. She's telling me a long and in-volved story about the ovarian cyst of someone I don't know. Charisma is boring me to tears and I keep yawning.

At a quarter past ten, someone who actually knows the person with the ovarian cyst and is asking interested ques-tions rescues me from Charisma.

I slide off the velvet cushion and start looking for Kate. I work my way down the hall and a girl with an English ac-cent and short spiky blond hair accosts me. She's wearing hot pants and a little sparkly top. She has glasses with very thick black frames. "Rachel! It is so-o-o good to see you!" says the funky hotpants girl.

I've never seen this person before in my life. "Hello . . ."

Oh dear, I don't know your name, that was definitely an "insert name here" type of hello, how can I cover?

"... there!" I say, grinning at her. "What have you been doing?"

Now, my understanding is that when someone asks "What have you been doing?" that is your cue to give a brief two- or three-sentence summary. For example, in my case it would be "Oh, you know, not much. I've moved out of home. I'm going to uni. I have a job." Thereafter, the asker can choose a topic area to pursue, it's like *Select a subject from the following menu.* This girl, however, took it as an invitation to tell me her whole life story. At least it was an interesting life story.

"Oh, well, as you know, I went to London as an exchange student."

Oh right! It's that dumpy-looking, quiet girl who went to London as an exchange student. What was her name?

"It was fabulous, just fabulous. It's changed my whole life."

I have never seen someone change so much. I can't believe my eyes! She used to be one of those girls who looked about forty! Now she is a thin, funky-looking person in hot pants. What was her name?

She goes on and on about the school she went to and how she traveled all across Europe and she came back to London and performed in a troupe of acrobats as a juggler. She went to the Edinburgh Fringe Festival, where she fell in love with a stand-up comic who ended up being bisexual and two months later ran off with her flatmate.

"I was just devastated. I mean, my flatmate who I had lived with for years, Nigel, we went to Madrid together and to Prague. And then Edinburgh, naturally. We had been the dearest of friends. Suddenly he started wanting his name to be pronounced 'Nee-gel.' I couldn't believe it. It was just so painful. So I said to myself, Ruth . . ."

Ruth! Her name was Ruth.

"I said to myself, Ruth, it's time to go home. I mean Europe is fantastic, of course, but I couldn't get far enough away from Nee-gel, and Australia is about as far as you can get, really, isn't it?"

Ruth tells me that she came back to Australia to start a degree in performing arts, but she's finding it really difficult. Not the degree part, naturally, because she has made a living out of performing arts, but the being back in Australia part.

"I'm living with my parents to save money. They're trying to run my life. I just can't wait to get back to Europe."

At eleven I leave Ruth, promising to catch up another day. I find Kate to say goodbye. She's fighting with Maxwell in the kitchen. Maxwell is standing at the back door, he has his coat over his arm and is playing with a set of car keys in his hand.

Where is *he going?*

She gives me a hug and we promise to have coffee.

I drive home to find Grace in bed asleep and Mr. Preston sitting on the couch with his head thrown back, snoring. I walk into the kitchen, put the kettle on and bang the kitchen cabinets for a bit, hoping he will wake up.

I walk into my bedroom and kick off my boots.

When I come back, Mr. Preston is awake. "Must have dozed off," he says with that startled look. His eyes are all red and glassy and his hair is standing up at a funny angle at the back. I offer him a cuppa but he says he'll just go home. He picks up the pizza boxes and takes them outside to the bin.

When he comes back in, he says to me, "Our mate next door came back from the police station earlier, and those two had one hell of a barney. All's quiet now, though."

He picks up his keys and his phone. "Did you have a nice time?"

I nod and smile brightly. "Yes. Thank you for coming over."

"No worries. It's good to see you're getting out a bit," he says, patting my shoulder.

He tiptoes to the front door, like some kind of pantomime burglar. "Well, good night then," he whispers.

"Good night."

He closes the door silently behind him.

I changed and hopped into bed. I lay for a while with the light on, thinking about Ruth and how different she was. I thought about how she went from a dumpy-looking nobody to a person who has done something exciting, all on her own in another country.

I wonder how much we change and adapt to our environment? Who would I be if I were not here? What if I had stayed at home? What would I be doing now? Has taking this job changed my destiny?

The big question is did Ruth become a juggler because she was in a juggler-friendly place, or was she fated always to be a juggler and sought a place to realize her destiny?

I thought about Grace, who had an exciting life and now . . .

I thought about how such dramatic changes are occurring in people's lives all around us, all the time. We plan, we think we know where we're going and then bang—we meet someone or we see things that change our whole life, just like that. Or do we invite the bang by the choices we make?

I lay under my quilt and shivered. Sentience, man! Who needs it? Life was much easier ten minutes ago when I knew everything.

Meanwhile, if Mr. Preston was the overcoat-wearer with the blue lips, how come he didn't pick it up when I called the cat Pritchard?

Curiouser and curiouser.

Tight Mouth came to see me today. Why? Why me?
I don't like her.

I was standing out in the back garden, watering. Plants
keep appearing. I don't know much about plants, but plants
seem to be appearing that I'm sure weren't there before.

There are several rosebushes that have healthy-looking
new growth on them. I'm very excited about the prospect of
roses. I will be able to fill the house with flowers.

Brioney sat on the edge of the pond. She told me she
wasn't speaking to Charity and she usually borrows her
sewing machine and would it be OK if she borrowed
Grace's for a couple of days?

I told her that Mr. Preston said I wasn't allowed to lend anything, but she was welcome to sew here if she liked.

Please, please, please don't say yes.

Brioney was sitting on the very edge of the pond with her long legs tucked primly sideways. "Well, all my patterns are at home and it really wouldn't be convenient. It really would be so much easier if I could take it with me. It would just be for the afternoon. Mr. Preston wouldn't have to know, now, would he?" she says, looking at me slyly.

"Brioney, you aren't suggesting that I would deceive my employer?"

She sniffed and shook her head briskly. "No, no, of course not."

She changed the subject. She told me that she was going to finish a quilt.

"I make quilts. I made one for Grace, you know. It's the one in your room. Months, it took me—months. Actually, I wouldn't mind taking it back, since she's not using it," she said, running her fingers through the back of her hair.

"I'm sort of using it at the moment," I said, smiling awkwardly.

"Oh." She shook her head briskly and sniffed. "I was going to come and pick it up while Grace was in hospital. Charity and I popped around to pick up a few things, you know, the valuable things, because it's not safe to leave them lying around, you know, with the house empty for who knows how long?"

She paused. Using her index finger, she pulled her gold necklace out from her shirt and ran her finger along its links, first to the left, then to the right. The loose folds of her skin around her throat stretched under the chain, first to the left, then to the right. It was disgusting and fascinating at the same time. Her tanned skin was dry and leathery, with little lines running through it, like a reptile's.

"When we came back the next time there was a security guard here. A security guard!"

Stretch left, stretch right. She had thin lips and they turned down at the sides.

She looks like a tortoise!

"Can you believe it? He wouldn't let us in the house! Her own sisters! I mean, I can understand protecting the house from burglars, but her own sisters! That's a bit over the top, don't you think?"

Her nose was turned up a little at the front so you could see the shape of her nostrils.

She looks exactly *like a tortoise! Oh, that's such a relief. It's been bugging me for ages.*

"Anyway, after a while he was only here at nights. The nurses were here on their own during the day, well, except for Grace, of course. Charity and I popped round a couple of times, to see if there were any valuables lying around. I mean, I know this nursing agency is very reputable and everything, but you can't trust anyone these days. Some young nurse, after a bit of extra cash, sees a gold bracelet lying around and . . . well, you know what I'm saying."

I can't look at her anymore. I'm afraid I'm going to laugh. I *do not* want to laugh.

"Charity and I were only trying to protect Grace's things. Mr. Preston thinks himself all high and mighty and orders everyone around. He told the nurses not to let us take anything and to call him directly if we came over. I don't know who he thinks he is."

You know what I reckon? Brioney is cross because she's the older sister. She thinks she should be running Grace's life, not Mr. Preston. She thinks it's her responsibility. She wants the responsibility because it makes her feel important.

You know what else I reckon? I reckon she always has been jealous of Grace for being attractive and the career woman in the family. I reckon she's angry because Grace was so independent and doesn't need Brioney, even now.

"Anyway, love, I better be off. I've got a class this evening."

Brioney left.

I watered the garden for a while longer, humming to myself. I should be a shrink, man. I know so much.

When I went back to my room, my quilt was gone.

i went to uni this afternoon. We had a prac. I'm really
getting into this uni lingo. When I walked into the lab, I
saw Hiro. He smiled at me, so I went and sat next to him. I
didn't have anything to say, so I let him talk to me.

When he started to speak, I couldn't understand him at
all. I could feel a blush creeping up my neck and chin, so I
leant forward on the desk and tucked my chin into my
elbow. I sort of cocked my head while he talked to me. I had
to listen really hard but once I got used to it I stopped
thinking about blushing. After a little while I had no trouble
understanding him at all.

It turns out his name isn't Hiro at all. It's Harold. He
comes from Taiwan. His father works in finance. He's doing

his degree here in Australia because you can get a better job in Taiwan if you have a degree from here.

He has a younger brother at home whom he misses very much. He likes to play soccer. He plays the cello.

The cello is a pretty cool instrument to play. My brother, Brody, played the euphonium in primary school. He wanted to play the saxophone but he was late to the first band rehearsal. The euphonium—the uncoolest of all the brass instruments—was all that was left. No kid dreams of being a concert euphoniumist, do they? Except of course, my brother. He practiced diligently.

Pwarp, pwarp, pwarp.

The euphonium has such an unromantic sound. There are never any euphonium solos. You never see "Concerto for Euphonium in C." So when my brother practiced, there was never any melody, just *pwarp, pwarp, pwarp, pause, pwarp.*

When he went to high school they didn't have any euphoniums, so he gave it up. They had an alto sax, but he wasn't interested.

Hiro was telling me about how he's learning to play the cello. He said he went to classes in Taiwan after school.

"My mother, she makes me practice, always. Now I am here, I don't practice so much. She phones me up, 'Are you practicing your cello?', 'Yes, Mum,' I say. But I don't practice so much as I say," he said, smiling.

I asked Hiro if he would like to go to the bar with me sometime. My head was bobbing up and down as I talked because my jaw was wedged into my elbow. He smiled and said that he would like that very much.

While we were doing the prac I noticed that he had

long muscular arms and beautiful strong hands. When he turned his head away from me to look at the blackboard, I noticed he had a really nicely defined jawline and a strong, muscly neck.

When he turned back to me, he smiled again. I felt butterflies in my belly.

Oh dear. I'm starting to notice curves about his person. I think I fancy him.

i think that Grace has started to respond to me. Just recently she has started to turn her head toward me when I walk into the room. Her eyes look through me. What I mean is, her eyes are looking at my eyes but it's as if she's focusing on something just behind me.

When I first arrived I found her creepy, but it's different now.

Tonight I was in Grace's study and I had just opened up the spooky box. I had the desk lamp on. I was settling in, feet up and reclining, like you do.

Some people say they can feel it when someone is watching them. I have never had that sensation. I'm just not psychic at all. I haven't got second sight, hearing or smell.

Wouldn't that be a weird psychic power? What would second smell be useful for, then?

Ommm, your great-great-grandmother wishes you to know that the secret ingredient is tarragon.

Ommm, fifty years ago somebody had cheese fondue in this room.

Ommm, some entity is frying chicken on another astral plane.

That would be the problem with second smell. How would you know you were having a psychic experience and not just smelling something?

So, I'm reclining and I look up and Grace is standing in the doorway watching me. She looks just like I imagined when I first arrived. Most people, when they are standing for any length of time, tend to lean on one foot, or lean against whatever is nearest. It's dark and Grace just stands there with her hands hanging straight down beside her and her bare feet together. Her face is all white, her bottom lip droops and she looks straight at me.

I'm reclining in the reclining chair, frozen. The light is coming from behind her, outlining her shape in the doorway. All I can see is her white face and her dark eyes.

I feel fright, but fright from not expecting her to be there rather than fright from Grace herself. This is just Grace, gentle Grace, silent Grace, Grace for whom I made peanut-butter soldiers this morning.

I stand up and walk over to her.

"What is it?" I ask, putting my hands on her shoulders.

Her dark eyes are on my face, sort of *through* my face. I'm standing in front of her. She opens her mouth.

Oh my God, she's going to speak.

I stand very still and wait for her to speak. My heart beats very fast, not with fear but excitement and anticipation.

I stood in front of her, waiting. Of course, she didn't speak. She just stood there looking through me with her mouth open. After a while I realized we had been standing there staring at each other for so long it was ridiculous. I turned her around and put her back to bed.

I lay in bed and I couldn't sleep. I wondered what I'd thought it was that she was going to say.

Get out of my spooky box and mind your own business. By the way, I really don't like peanut-butter soldiers.

I lay there and wondered if she would ever speak again. What would her first words be?

Something terrible happened today. Grace has with-drawn again. She wet herself again this afternoon, after we got home. She hasn't done that for ages. She has gone back down again. Whatever was coming out in her has gone. I look into her eyes and there is nothing. She has stopped looking at me again.

I went to university this morning. I was in the lecture theater. Hiro isn't in this class, so I sat by myself. There was a boy sitting in front of me with this giant bottle of water. Every now and then he would take a long leisurely sip.

All of a sudden I was thirstier than I have ever been in my life. My mouth was dry, my throat was dry, my skin was dry. I felt as if I'd just eaten a salt sandwich on stale bread with soy sauce. I couldn't think, because every nerve in my body was saying *thirsty, thirsty, thirsty*. I looked at this giant bottle of water in front of me that I couldn't have.

I had to leave. I packed up my stuff and walked out of the lecture theater. I had to have a drink.

I walked down to the coffee shop and there was Kate with a whole bunch of herbal-looking people. She was sitting cross-legged on the chair—force of habit, I assume. She waved me over. I took a big bottle of water out of the fridge and paid for it.

I sat down with Kate and her friends. They remembered me from the party. I couldn't remember their names.

"OK, what I want to know is how much of my destiny is predetermined," I said as I sat down.

"Well," said Kate, without blinking an eye, "I think it's a combination of choice and fate."

Kate held her mug of coffee delicately in her lap.

"I disagree," said a blond surfer type with dreadlocks. "We are all part of a swirling cosmos. Everything connects —that's nature. You know if a butterfly flaps its wings in South America—"

"Don't give me that," interrupted a pert-looking girl with a red skivvy on, "you're confusing correlation with co-incidence."

The cafeteria buzzed with conversation and laughter. Cleaning ladies in pale blue tunics wandered from table to table collecting dirty plates and stacking them on industrial-looking trolleys.

The pert girl looked at me over the rim of her coffee cup. "You go ahead and create your own destiny, pet. Don't listen to him. He's an environmental science major."

"No, you didn't let me finish," said the boy with dread-locks, "it's basic physics. Every action has an equal and op-posite reaction."

"So, what's equal about a wing flap and a meteorological disaster of biblical proportions, you goose?" argued the pert girl.

At the table nearest to us a group of young men erupted with laughter. The dreadlock boy had to raise his voice to be heard above them.

"You can't tell me that Nature doesn't have a plan," he said. "Let's look at the basic principle of survival of the fittest. You can't tell me that—"

"Yes, but who's talking about Nature? We live in a mod-ern society—an artificial structure that supports the weak," interrupted the pert girl. "It's one of the critical factors un-derpinning our civilization, you twerp."

The boy with the dreadlocks put down the glass bottle he had been drinking from. "Firstly, we are still animals," he said, shaking his head and pointing his finger. "We are not immune to the forces of Nature. And secondly, I object to your constant insults, which clearly indicate a flimsy argu—"

Sitting between them, Kate and I swiveled our heads from one to the other like tennis spectators.

"Oh, get out of my face," said the pert girl. She turned her head away and waved her hand at him. "We live in a so-ciety where limbs are replaceable and barren women are as-sisted to bear children. Tell me that isn't a huge step toward immunity."

The dreadlock boy took a deep breath and was about to speak when I interrupted. "OK, let's say that I go to Edin-

burgh and become a juggler. Is that fate or coincidence?"
I asked.

"Oh, you mean Ruth?" said Kate. "Well, that's different.
She definitely heard the call of the juggler within."

"No doubt about it," said the pert girl.

"Yes," agreed the dreadlock boy, "Ruth is a predestined
juggler. She would have been a juggler even if she lived in
Brewarrina."

They paused for a moment. A cleaner with trolley
leaned toward us, collecting plates and bottles from our
table.

"How prometropolitan are you?" said the pert girl, as
the cleaning lady moved away. "Are you suggesting that
someone who lives in a remote or regional area can't have
aspirations in the field of performing arts?"

"No," replied the dreadlock boy. "Just that opportunities to pursue different occupations are locality-based."

"Don't listen to him," said the pert girl, leaning toward
me and placing her hand on my arm, "he's from Cronulla."

"Now who's being locationalist? I'm just saying that
you're going to have a hard time being a marine biologist if
you live in Alice," said the dreadlock boy.

"Which brings me back to my original question," I said.
"Are you a marine biologist *because* you live by the sea, or do
you live by the sea *because* you are a marine biologist?"

Kate smiled at me and said, "I think it's a combination
of choice and fate."

I'd finished guzzling my water so I said goodbye to Kate
and her friends and meandered home across the park. I
thought about having just missed my first lecture. I couldn't

believe it. I wondered if I should go back. What if they'd talked about something really important that was going to be in the exam? One lecture, surely one lecture doesn't matter? As long as I read what's in the textbook I'll be right.

I walked along the cycleway through the park. A cyclist zipped up behind me, ringing his little bell. How can anyone be taken seriously with a wee bell like that?

Ting, ting, everybody move! Ting, ting.

Quick, quick. Everybody move out of the way! There is a thin person in Lycra, on a lightweight aluminum frame with flimsy wheels.

Cyclists should have a gong. I'm sure people would have more respect for them if they had a gong. Also, it would help if they didn't shave their legs. Please? How much quicker do they honestly think that makes them? If your leg hair is so long that it's getting caught in your spokes, fair enough. I can see how that would make a difference. Otherwise, I'm just not convinced.

I mean, just take a look at animals for whom speed really matters: African big cats, for example, zebras, antelopes. They all have hair! How many lions does one see saying, "Damn, I could have caught that wildebeest, if only it wasn't for these blasted hairy legs!"

So, I'm walking along the cycleway in the park. I'm thinking I might go grocery shopping. The only thing in the cupboard is a tin of artichoke hearts. I don't know any recipes that use artichoke hearts.

I think it's time to shop.

So, when I get home I take Grace to the supermarket. We were doing the grocery shopping. We were at the counter. I would hand things to Grace—things out of the trolley and she would put them on the counter—not the heavy things. She was doing really well. I was talking to her, making encouraging noises. People standing around must think I'm a dill.

Anyway, I'd forgotten to get dishwashing liquid. She was doing so well and the queue behind us was really long. It was only two aisles away, so I left her on her own. I decided I'd just duck over and grab the dishwashing liquid. I'd be back in two seconds. All she had to do was just stand there, right? Stupid, I know, in hindsight. I should know by now not to leave her on her own.

Anyway, I left her standing there. I rushed down to the aisle with the dishwashing liquid. Maybe she got frightened, maybe she was just wandering about looking for me? Who knows?

I came out of the aisle and I could see what was happening. It was as if it were in slow motion. She was walking through the checkout. The lady behind the counter was saying "Hey, come back, you'll set off the—" It was as if I can see the words coming out of her mouth, and I'm watching as Grace walks through the alarm doorway thing. She's got a bottle of cranberry juice in her hand. I can still see her walking, head swiveling as she's looking for me, still hear the checkout chick, when the alarm goes off, "REEP, REEP, REEP." You know that really earsplitting sound like someone screaming.

I'm standing there at the end of the aisle. I can see Grace's eyes, opening very wide as she spins around.

Panic.

I can see as she drops the bottle of cranberry juice, her

147

mouth open, she puts her hand up to her ears. The bottle falls on the floor and shatters in a million pieces. The cranberry juice is flowing all over the floor.

I start running toward her, but there are all these trolleys in the way and all these people moving closer to see what's going on. I'm yelling, trying to sound soothing over the sound of this alarm. "It's all right, turtledove."

I'm pushing people and trolleys out of the way, they're all moving closer to the commotion. I can't get to her. I feel as if I'm on a conveyor belt that's going the other way.

I'm watching and I see a security guard approaching from behind Grace.

No, don't touch her!

He grabs her by the upper arm. She didn't see him approaching and she struggles to get away from him. She slips on the cranberry juice and falls. I can see her eyes.

Panic.

She falls on the floor and she's sliding along, her arms and hands sliced up by the broken glass on the floor. I'm still running—still trying to get past the stupid trolleys. The alarm's going "REEP, REEP!" The guard leans forward and grabs her arm again, hauling her to her feet and she's struggling, making these little squeaky noises.

There's blood dripping down her arm. The guard is shouting at her. "Just settle down, love, just settle down."

She pulls away from the guard and falls again. I can see a big chunk of glass sticking out of her calf. I shove my way through the people, really pushing them out of the way, and burst my way through the checkout like a cannonball. I throw my arms around her in a bear hug.

I'm here, I'm here, I'm here.

I hold her, whispering in her ear. "It's OK, turtledove, it's OK. I'm here." I'm sitting there on the floor wrapped around Grace and she's shaking all over. We're covered in blood and cranberry juice. Sitting there on the floor, I'm rocking her gently. She's shuddering and taking big gulping breaths.

●　●　●

Well, I won't be leaving her on her own anymore.

The security guard at the shopping center has wrapped up Grace's arms and leg in bandages. I drive Grace to the hospital. A nurse takes her away into a little room. I phone Mr. Preston from the public telephone in the foyer.

"I'm at the hospital," I say. I coil the phone wire around and around my wrist as I'm talking.

"What's happened?"

"I left her on her own, just for a second, in the supermarket. She fell over and cut herself."

There is silence on the other end of the line.

"How bad?"

"Pretty bad."

"I'll be right there."

I'm sitting in the foyer, forever. I've got a magazine open on my lap but I'm not reading it.

Mr. Preston comes running into the foyer. He sees me and walks over. "Where's Grace?"

"She's in there," I say, pointing to the little room. I put my hands up to my face and start to cry. "I'm so sorry. It's my fault. I left her on her own. I went to get dishwashing liquid. It's my fault."

He sits down on the plastic chair next to me and puts his arm around my shoulder. He pulls me toward him and kisses me on the top of my head. Then he stands up and walks into the little room.

Mr. Preston drives Grace home. One of her legs and both her arms are in bandages. At home I sit her in her chair. Mr. Preston makes us a cup of coffee. We sit in silence on the couch.

Eventually I say, "Would you like me to resign?"

Mr. Preston frowns at me. "Grace has just made a payment, in flesh, toward your education. You don't think we're going to start all over again with someone else?"

I feel bad. I feel very bad.

We are silent again.

He finishes his coffee. "Well, I think it's time to go home. It's been a big day." He stands up and takes my cup out of my hand. He walks into the kitchen. "I was having coffee with my ex-wife when you rang. We're very civilized, you see. Sometimes the civility can be . . . stressful."

I can't think of anything to say.

Mr. Preston walks over to Grace, kneels down before her and holds her hands. He speaks to her quietly, but I can hear him.

"Well, now, you gave us quite a fright today. I'm going now. Please be gentle with my little chum. We can't have her beating herself up, as well."

He kisses her hands and walks to the front door.

On the veranda I say to him, "I'm so sorry. I will never leave her on her own again. I wasn't thinking. I did the wrong thing."

He nods. He scuffs the sole of his shoes on the edge of the step. He puts his hands on his hips. "The garden is looking good," he observes.

"I've let you down. I wasn't doing my job. Now Grace is a mess and it's my fault."

I look at him closely. There are tears in his eyes. He stands on the veranda, looking at the garden.

I can't believe he's crying. He's a grown-up, for heaven's sake!

"I am so sorry," I say.

"Shut up for a minute, will you? Grace's cuts will heal. Do you hear me? You're doing a fantastic job."

Then he turns and looks me right in the eye.

"I know where you are right now. You're blaming yourself. Well, I can trump that. I was there the night Grace had the accident. That was my fault. How does that grab you?"

Two tears roll down his cheeks.

"Grace's cuts will heal. What I did she will never recover from—never, ever." He pulls his hair back from his forehead with both hands and rubs his eyes. "I tell myself she was at the wrong place at the wrong time, but the truth is, I took her to that place. I took them both there."

He takes a handkerchief out of his pocket and wipes his eyes.

"I have to go."

He walks down the steps to his car. He turns back toward me as he opens the car door.

"Your trial is over, by the way."

Then he drives away, without looking back.

24

We picked up Prickles this morning and we brought him home in a pillowcase on Grace's lap. I haven't let Grace out of my sight. She hasn't looked at me once since the supermarket.

Marie gave me some pills for Prickles and some special food. She told me that he's going to be sore for a couple of weeks, but he'll be fine.

When we got home I pulled him out of the pillowcase and put him on the floor. He lay there for a while on his side, and I could see his naked little belly, where they'd shaved him, and a big line of stitches.

I picked him up gently and put him on Grace's lap. She looked down and stroked him along his back.

I sat on the couch looking at them: Grace with her arms and leg in bandages, Prickles with his stitches all the way up his belly—what a pair.

Yeah, I'm doing a fantastic job. Australia's number one primary carer, that's me.

I locked the front and back doors and walked into the study and pulled out the spooky box. For a while I sat at the desk just looking at the box. I felt bad. I felt voyeuristic, but I couldn't help myself, I wanted to know more.

I could have put it away but I opened it instead. I pulled out the bundle that I'd already read and picked up the next piece of paper. It was written in crayon in a childish hand. There was a drawing—a kid's drawing with a big yellow smiling sun in the corner. I sat there at Grace's desk and read.

Dear Aunty Grace,

Thank you for taking me to the zoo when Mummy was sick. I liked the monkeys best.

I told Daddy how you taught me to play the piano.

You'll never guess what. When I came home I had a new sister! Her name is Bianca.

Can I come and stay again?

I told Aunty Brioney you make better cakes than her.

Love from Simone

PS I drawed you a picture of us at the zoo with the monkeys.

I smiled as I put the picture under the ribbon. I just bet Brioney would love being told Grace makes better cakes than she does.

I heard the floorboards in the hallway creak. I put the lid on the box and left it sitting on the desk.

Grace was standing at the front door, looking straight ahead, her nose a few centimeters away from the wood. I looked up the hallway. Prickles was sitting on Grace's chair, licking his stitches and looking sorry for himself.

"Do you want to go outside?"

I moved her back from the door and opened it. As she stepped out on the veranda, I could hear a voice saying, "There you are, Miss Grace! We haven't seen you for donkey's! How you been keeping?"

Two old men were standing at the gate. They were both wearing hats. They had old men's shirts on with the two pleated pockets at the front. They had socks pulled up all the way to their knees and sensible beige walking shoes.

I should point out that they looked like a pair of clowns. They looked as if they stepped straight out of a black-and-white movie. There was something extraordinarily Marxesque about their getups, I have to say.

"Well, looks to me like someone's come a buster, what do you reckon, Herb?" says the first man.

"Herb" laughs as he reaches into his baggy shorts pocket, pulling out a pouch of tobacco. He picks out a paper and sticks it to his lip. He takes out a pinch of tobacco, puts it in the paper and tucks the pouch back in his pocket.

The other man looks up at me and pokes his hat to the back of his head with one finger. "Well, hello there. We've been worried about the little fellow. We was walking past and thought we might inquire about his health."

"The little fellow?"

"Miss Grace's little chap. He normally comes up pretty regular, you know? We haven't seen him about."

"You mean Prickles," I say.

"That's the little fellow. Prickles. That's what I said, Herb, Prickles."

Herb lights his cigarette with a match, shielding the flame with his old gnarled hand. "No you didn't, Bill, you was calling him Patches," he says, shaking the match out.

"No I wasn't! Why would I call him that, eh? He doesn't have no patches!"

"Yes you was, Bill. You said, 'Haven't seen Patches about for a couple of days,' I remember it clear as a bell, in my memory it is." Herb taps his forehead with his middle finger.

"I'm Rachel," I say.

They look up at me. "Well, how do you do, Rachel. I'm Herb and this is Bill. We live on up the road a stretch." Herb points up the road with one arthritically bent finger. He takes a drag and then nods. "Like I said, Patches normally comes up regular, he sits on our porch in the sun and we give him our scraps."

"Now you're at it, Herb! They call him Prickles, not Patches."

"That's what I said."

"No you didn't, you called him Patches."

"No I didn't, why would I call him Patches? He don't have no patches." Herb winks at me. His hand is on the gate, the cigarette smoke winding up lazily around his wrist. "See, Miss Rachel, Bill don't hear as well as he used to."

"Prickles has been at the vet's, he's had an operation," I say.

"Had a spill, has he?" asks Herb.

"The man next door kicked him in the stomach."

Bill and Herb shake their heads. "Nothing but trouble, those two," Bill says.

"Well, it's nice to see someone's taking a bit of care of this garden again. We was walking past not so long ago and I said to Bill, 'It's a crying shame no one's taking care of that garden, after all the work what Miss Grace put in,' didn't I, Bill? A crying shame. Many's a time Bill and I'd come down here and give her a few pointers. Didn't we, Miss Grace?"

"That's right, Miss Rachel," Bill says, taking his hat off and rubbing his bald head with the heel of his hand. "We'd come down here and Miss Grace would be here in this garden pruning or watering or what have you. We'd stop for a spell and chat about this and that. More often than not, Herb would stroll up to our place and bring us all back a couple of nice coldies."

Herb rolls another cigarette. "We'd be telling her stories of when we was boys and she'd laugh. Didn't she have a nice laugh, Bill?"

"Yep."

The two men stand looking at the garden.

"That puts me in mind, Herb. Why don't you stroll up and fetch us some coldies now?"

"Do you fancy a cold one now, Miss Rachel?" says Herb.

"Well now, Herb, I think I do."

"Do you think Miss Grace would fancy a coldie?" Herb asks me.

"I think she probably would," I reply, smiling.

Herb strolled up the road to fetch us some "coldies."

Grace and I sat down in the chairs on the veranda. Bill perched himself on the top step, fanning his face with his hat. "Well now, Miss Grace, isn't this just like old times, eh? Them petunias have picked up again, now, haven't they?"

Herb walked back down the street with four beers in his hands.

We sat there until sunset, Herb occasionally taking a stroll to fetch us another. Herb and Bill told me stories from when they were boys, when people used to buy their milk and fruit and vegetables from horse-drawn carts on this street. They told me horror stories about working in the mines forty years ago. They told me about Grace.

"She made a real decent pie. On occasion Miss Grace would bake too much for herself," Herb said. "She'd bring us out some tucker all wrapped up in a tea towel. She made a real decent pie. We'd take it home and have it for our tea."

"She may not have been real strong on horticulture, but she made a decent pie," agreed Bill.

We sat quietly for a moment. Herb rubbed his face with his callused hands, making a scratchy noise.

Prickles limped out of the house and climbed into Bill's lap and they tut-tutted about his injuries.

"We was looking after Patches for a stretch," said Herb. "He was coming up to our place, carrying on, playing up merry hell. We didn't know what had happened. We came down here and Miss Grace wasn't about."

"We was starting to get a bit worried about her," continued Bill. "We came down and chatted for a spell with the security man who was stationed here. He told us Miss Grace had had herself a stroke or some such."

"Terrible thing to happen to someone so young," said Herb.

"Terrible," said Bill. "This is the first time we've really seen Miss Grace since then, except passing by."

"Did Grace have many visitors?" I asked.

"Well, now, there was her sisters and their kids," said Bill, "they came around pretty regular, didn't they, Herb?"

Herb nodded. "Then there was a couple of young ladies on and off. And there was her mother. She was a real lady, was Grace's mother, God bless her. Brought Grace up with a real jolt when she passed on."

"What happened?" I asked.

"She was on holidays up the coast like they always was about that time of year," said Bill. "They had family up there, didn't they, Herb?"

"That's right, Grace had family up the coast somewhere and they was on the way to see them. Her father fell asleep at the wheel, I believe."

"No," said Bill, "you great goat! A young fella, not long had his driving ticket, careered into them on a corner."

"Anyways, they had a crash and passed on. Grace was real shook up. Her mum and her was real close," added Bill.

We sat quietly for a moment. I thought about the postcard from Grace's mother. All of a sudden I felt very sad.

"The young boy of Preston was here often enough, although I've never had much time for him," said Bill.

"Too clever by half," agreed Herb.

"Fancies himself a bit of a man about town," said Bill.

I was surprised, but kept quiet. This didn't sound like the Mr. Preston I knew. Maybe he has mellowed.

As the streetlights flickered on, Bill and Herb got to

their feet. "Well, now, Miss Rachel, thank you for your hospitality, but it's getting on time for our tea," said Herb.

They tipped their hats and strolled off up the street.

I brought Grace inside and sat her on the couch to watch television while I cooked dinner. I grilled some lamb cutlets and painted them with honey and soy sauce and sprinkled them with rosemary. I cut the meat off the bone and chopped it up into bite-sized pieces. I put the bones on my plate. I laid the pieces of meat on a bed of lettuce. We sat together at the dining table.

I fed Grace first because I thought her arms might be hurting. The nurse would be in tomorrow to change the dressing.

After dinner I sat Grace on the couch, putting her sore leg up on the coffee table. I was exhausted. We started to watch a movie.

I was thinking about the things that Bill and Herb had told me. I thought about Grace's mother. I wondered how she felt when she got that postcard. She would have already heard that they were dead. How awful.

I gave Grace a little hug. "I'm so sorry, Gracey."

I woke up at one o'clock. I was still on the couch. Grace was asleep next to me. The television was blaring infomercials. I woke Grace up and led her to her bedroom and put her into bed.

As I tucked her in I asked her, "Do you miss your mum?"

Grace was asleep.

Looking through the wardrobe, I could see the spooky box on the desk.

Just one and then I'm going to bed.

I reached into the box and pulled out two sheets of paper that were stuck to each other.

Just two and then I'm going to bed.

I sat in the recliner chair and read.

Yvonne,

I can't sleep. I dream about you off and on. This time I'm going to write. I could be dramatic and say it's the last time and give you some kind of ultimatum but I'm not going to do that.

I'll write to you again. I'll write again when my subconscious stirs me from my slumber—taps me on the shoulder and reminds me of what I've lost.

I knew you when you were five years old and we used to play hide-and-seek. One day you were hiding and you knocked over the bookshelf in your father's study and that big dictionary came down and knocked me unconscious.

I knew you when you were ten and you had a boil on your bum and you had to take a pillow to school. You made me take a pillow to school too, so you wouldn't be embarrassed.

I knew you when you were nineteen. I knew you so well when you were nineteen that the day we caught the Manly ferry from Circular Quay we changed the rules in Twenty Questions to five questions because that's as many questions as it took for us to know exactly what the other was thinking.

I don't know you today.

I don't know where you are. I don't know what you do in your leisure time. I don't know your family.

All of these things make me sad.

I think if we saw each other again we wouldn't know what to say. Isn't that a sorry state of affairs?

I just wanted you to know that I remember and I miss you.

If you need me you know where I am.

Love,

Grace

Dear Mrs. Preston,

I am writing in regard to your letter dated 14th October.

Yours is not the first letter that I have received of this nature. You might describe it as an occupational hazard. However, yours is the first that I have dignified with a response.

I thank you indeed for your suggestions as to what I can "stick up my snobby, posh twat." I was amused. I shall use some of those insults myself, if I may, should I ever run out of my own. I do believe, however, that your venom is misdirected.

While I have undergone some preliminary psychological training, I don't believe I am adequately qualified to counsel you. You are quite clearly delusional, and while I think it is very sweet that you believe your husband to be so captivating that I would be attracted to him, and flattering that you believe he is unable to resist my alleged "temptations," you may wish to consider seeking professional guidance.

Have you considered discussing your anxieties with your husband? Maybe you should contemplate communicating your apprehension with him? Do you feel that you *cannot discuss openly your feelings and your fears with him? If this is the case, is this really a relationship with which you wish to persevere?*

I can only encourage you to surround yourself with a nice caring circle of friends. Perhaps you could immerse yourself in a stimulating hobby?

Yours truly,

Grace

I rolled the two pieces of paper in my fingers. I was so tired that my legs were aching. My legs always ache when I'm overtired. I looked at my watch. It was half-past one in the morning. What was I doing up so late?

I tucked the letters under the ribbon with the other things I had read. I pushed the spooky box back in its spot behind the books. I walked back through the wardrobe to my bedroom.

I had a friend like Yvonne. She lived next door to me when I was little. It was in that magical time before school when there was nothing at all you had to do unless your mother said so. I would go over to Anna's place straight after breakfast and watch cartoons. We made cubbies out of cardboard cartons and played dress-up with my mother's old clothes. Her family moved away.

I thought about Yvonne and felt bad about the way I had spoken to her. I was so cold. I didn't know who she was.

I wonder what Anna is doing now?

25

i opened my eyes and looked at the clock. It felt like only about five minutes, but it was actually eight hours later. I had slept in again. I jumped out of bed, ran into Grace's room and took her to the toilet.

There was a knock at the door. I answered it in my jammy jams, peeking out through the space allowed by the chain between the door and the jamb.

It was Mr. Preston, holding a shopping bag. He held it up to me. "Morning, chum. I thought I would come over and cook breakfast for our invalids."

While he was cooking breakfast I had a long shower with the door closed. It is so nice to have a long shower. It's nice to have the door closed. Since I have been here I have only had short showers with the door open so I could hear if Grace needed me.

I dried my hair and dressed in jeans and a T-shirt. I came out of my room just as Mr. Preston was serving up fried bacon, eggs and tomatoes. "That smells delicious," I said, grabbing the plunger of coffee and my plate and carrying them to the paved area out the back. The sun was shining down through the creeping vine.

I fetched Grace, and Mr. Preston came out behind me, carrying a tray with the remaining two plates and the cups. We sat down together. Mr. Preston cut up Grace's breakfast into chunks and handed her the fork. She stabbed one of the chunks with her fork and put it in her mouth.

"I'm sorry about the other day. I didn't mean to burden you with my troubles," he said, piling a huge amount onto his fork.

"That's no problem," I said. "You told me you had a bad day."

"Yes, I think I told you I met up with my ex-wife."

"You said that you find that stressful."

Mr. Preston chewed for a while, frowning.

"She's doing very well and I'm happy for her."

"Do you have kids together?" I asked, grinding some pepper onto my breakfast.

"No. She's pregnant now, though." He poured the coffee. "My wife, that is, my ex-wife, is a wonderful woman. We met"—Mr. Preston looked up and looked me directly in the eye—"we met at university. I was studying law, of course, my father wouldn't have it any other way. She was studying arts. We got along well immediately. We had a large circle of friends. We went to parties together and we went to the theater together. We discussed literature. We agreed about most things. After three years, we still agreed about most things, so I went to see her father and asked for her hand." Mr. Preston paused for a moment to take a mouthful.

"We got married on a beautiful autumn day in a church, and went to the Greek islands for our honeymoon."

Mr. Preston stopped to take another mouthful.

"We bought a house and we both worked. When I was earning enough, she gave up her job and stayed at home. She cooked fabulous meals for my business associates. She went to art classes and filled our house with wonderful watercolors and tapestries and that kind of thing." Mr. Preston took a slurp of his coffee and refilled our cups from the jug.

"Every night I would come home and we would sit down and talk about my day and then we would talk about her day and everything was lovely."

Mr. Preston shoved his heaped fork into his mouth.

"One day I went to work and Grace was at her desk and she was crying. I asked her what was wrong and she said that she'd been driving to work and she'd seen an ambulance and she pulled over and the car in front of her pulled over and the ambulance passed them."

Mr. Preston paused for a moment, staring out past the end of the pavers to the garden.

"She said that she suddenly thought about how when someone is in danger or is hurt that an ambulance is called and that everyone moves so that the paramedics can get to that person in the shortest time possible. She said that all of a sudden she realized how wonderful that was. We, all of us, in this society, move so that someone we've never met can get help. Then she burst into tears again." Mr. Preston scraped the egg off the bottom of his plate with his knife and wiped it on the last piece of toast.

"I sat there on the edge of the desk and watched this woman crying uncontrollably, so vulnerable. Here was a woman who I'd thought was as tough as old boots just moved to tears by the most simple thing. And all of a sudden I felt an incredible wrench in my chest. I felt an urgent, frantic need to look after her and care for her."

Mr. Preston put his knife and fork together and pushed the plate away. He took a handkerchief out of his pocket and wiped his hands and his mouth with it.

"I loved my wife, she was my friend and we had good times together, but at that moment I knew the feeling I had when Grace cried was the strongest emotion I'd ever had in my life. Have you ever been in love?"

I shook my head. I've had crushes, but that's not the same thing.

He reached over and picked up Grace's plate and put it in front of him. He started to pick at the bits of bacon left over.

"You know that song by Melanie C? It's called 'Never Be the Same Again.' She talks about a friendship that changes into something more. It's a beautiful song. That's how I felt. I just wanted to be there when she felt sad, I wanted to be the one who would make her happy again. I just wanted to be wherever she was."

Mr. Preston scraped the remains of Grace's breakfast onto his fork with the knife.

"I thought about her all the time. I couldn't help it.

I would walk in the street and I would see a florist and I would think of Grace. I would buy a bunch of flowers and I would take them home to my wife, and she would say, 'How thoughtful,' but I knew, when I gave them to her, that the person I had been thinking of was Grace, and I felt bad about that." He took another slurp of coffee.

"A year later I was still buying flowers for Grace and giving them to my wife. I knew it wasn't just a passing infatuation. I wished that it had been. I still wanted to be where Grace was and I felt it more and more strongly. I told my wife that while I loved her and I cared for her, I didn't want to spend the rest of my life with her, and then she cried."

Mr. Preston took another slurp of his coffee.

"I felt sad, too, because we had shared a great many things together. She asked me if there was someone else, and I hesitated. My wife took that as a yes. I tried to explain, but I knew that I was only hurting her more."

Mr. Preston put Grace's now-empty plate onto his own. "Are you going to eat that?" he said, pointing to my plate. I shook my head. Mr. Preston leaned over and picked up my plate and put it in front of him. Then he continued, "I left. She kept that house and I moved into a unit that we had in the city. We meet for coffee every now and then. She is seeing someone else. They're going to have a baby."

We sat silently for a moment.

"You see now it's a hopeless case. I love Grace. I have tried to meet other people and while they may be nice or pretty or clever, I find myself comparing them always to Grace, and that's not fair. I shall never be happy with anyone else. She is the one for me—end of story."

Mr. Preston smiled wryly.

"So now I spend my days hoping that one day she will be herself again and knowing that she probably won't."

Mr. Preston cleaned up the rest of my plate. He is silent because he's finished the story. I am silent because I am stunned.

I can't believe Mr. Preston knows the lyrics of songs by Melanie C.

Jan poked her head through the doorway from the living room, nearly giving me a heart attack.

"Hello there! I knocked, but there was no answer. I figured you must be out here. Hello, Mr. Preston, I didn't see you there. Just missed breakfast, have I? Oh, well, never mind, eh?"

Mr. Preston piled all the plates on the tray. "Can I get you coffee?"

"Oh, yes, please, darl. That would be lovely."

"More coffee, chum?" asked Mr. Preston over his shoulder, as he carried the tray inside.

"Yes, please."

"Well now," said Jan, sitting down and adjusting her

uniform, "how's our patient today? I understand we've got some dressings to change?"

Mr. Preston came back with a fresh jug of coffee, and we sat outside for a while longer. Mr. Preston made small talk with Jan while we finished our coffees. I walked back inside to do the dishes while Jan changed Grace's dressings. Mr. Preston watched for a while and then helped dry up.

I looked at the clock. Time to go to uni. I left Mr. Preston and Jan sitting on the couch chatting and walked through the park.

I arrived at my class and sat down next to Hiro. The lecturer reminded us that we had an assignment due in a week. I asked Hiro if he would like to come over to my house and work on the assignment with me. Of course, I blushed furiously, but I got through it.

He smiled at me and said he would like that very much. I felt those shivers in my belly again. I wrote down the address and handed it to him. Our hands touched for a second. I felt electricity streaking up my arm.

Oooh, Hiro. Lay your love on me.

We agreed that I would go to the library and borrow some books and we would meet at my place in the afternoon.

I skipped home across the park singing.

Jan was ready to go when I arrived. "You look bright and chirpy this afternoon, darl," she said with a twinkle in her eye. "Your mother rang before."

I ran into the bathroom and put some makeup on and brushed my hair. I ran out again and looked from the front veranda.

Not here yet—good.

I ran around the house, picking up nonexistent pieces of fluff off the floor. I brushed Grace's hair and washed her face. I ran out onto the front veranda again.

Not here yet—good.

I ran into the kitchen and wrenched open the fridge. I took down a glass jug from the cupboard and filled it with ice-cold water from the fridge. I sliced up a lemon and threw it in the jug. I pulled three glasses out of the cupboard and wiped them with the tea towel until they were sparkling.

I ran out onto the front veranda.

I could see Hiro wandering along the street with his bag hung over one shoulder, the other hand in the pocket of his baggy shorts.

I ran back into the bathroom to check on my makeup and my hair. I flew out of the bathroom and hurled myself on the couch. I lay there with one hand behind my head, looking casual.

I heard Hiro open the front gate. I could hear his footfall on the path, up the stairs and onto the veranda. He knocked on the door.

I lay on the couch with my heart thumping in my chest.

Don't want to appear too eager. One elephant, two elephant, three elephant.

I stood up and poked my head down the hallway.

"Oh, hello!" I said, trying to sound as if I had forgotten he was coming. "Come in."

Hiro sauntered down the hallway and threw his bag on the couch.

"This is a very nice home," he said, smiling that beautiful, wide, friendly smile.

"Oh, yes . . ."

Think of something witty to say, think of something witty to say.

My mind was a blank. We stood in the living room beaming at each other.

"Won't you come and sit down? I'll just grab a drink." I pulled one of the dining chairs out, casually, as I walked past. It caught on the edge of the carpet and fell over backward.

I picked the chair up and did a silly little jig thing that I can't bear to think about.

I walk toward him to the kitchen. At the same time, he walks toward me to sit in the chair. We find ourselves standing about fifty centimeters apart. I move to the right, he moves to the right. I move to the left, he moves to the left. I find myself doing one of those stilted bush-dance moves we were forced to do in physical education.

"Do the do-si-do," I shout. I skip around him. Of course they don't do-si-do in Taiwan so as I'm moving backward dancing feverishly, I run into him and knock him onto the couch. He lies there looking surprised.

I can't bear to think about it.

As I am standing there looking at him flailing about on the couch, I can feel a huge blush coming. I run into the kitchen and shove my head in the fridge to hide my blush.

It's not going away! The blush is not going away!

I take out the jug of water. I'm trying to keep my back to him. I step back and feel something squishy under my foot. I move back another step and run into him again, because he's standing right behind me. I look down and bang into

174

him with my bottom. Fresh hot streaks of blush flood into my cheeks.

The squishy thing is his foot. He's trying to move backward, but I'm still standing on his foot so he falls over again.

This is going very badly.

I step off his foot but get tangled in his other leg. I fall over. I've still got the jug in my hand and as I'm falling I pour the ice-cold water and the lemons onto Hiro.

This is going very, very, very badly.

We're sitting on the kitchen floor in a heap. Our legs are tangled up. Hiro is drenched. He's got a piece of lemon on his shoulder.

I start to laugh. He starts to laugh. We roll around on the kitchen floor holding our bellies and laughing.

I look up and Grace is standing in the living room looking at us.

I stand up and put my hand out to help Hiro up. He smiles at me. "Can I trust you?" he asks me. I pull him up and he shakes the water out of his hair.

Oh, oh, oh, I want to hear you say, I love ya, uh ha.

I introduce Hiro to Grace. He puts his hand out. He looks surprised and embarrassed when she looks the other way.

"Grace is brain-damaged," I explain to him.

"Oh . . . what happened?" he asks me.

"She had an accident."

"What kind of accident?"

I look at him blankly. "I don't know. I have never asked."

I can hear Bill's voice in my head. *"She had had herself a stroke or some such."*

I've never asked!

I move Grace over to her chair. Prickles limps in the back door.

"The cat had an accident, too?" Hiro asks me.

"Yes," I say as I pick Prickles up and put him gently on Grace's lap.

"Everyone has had an accident around you," he says, frowning.

This strikes me as hilariously funny. What, does he think I'm some kind of female version of Frank Spencer? Does he think I gave Grace brain damage and ruptured the cat's guts (*oowa Betty*) in some kind of sitcom slapstick routine? I start to laugh again. Hiro looks at me, perplexed. I'm doubled over, holding my stomach. Hiro starts to smile and soon he is laughing too.

When we had recovered, we sat at the dining table and worked on our assignment for about an hour. When Hiro concentrated he would frown and poke his tongue out a little bit.

After we had finished our assignment, we sat out in the back under the shade of the creeper. He put his leg up on the seat next to him. I could see the muscle in his calf flex and relax, flex and relax.

I was mesmerized.

"I first noticed the smell is very different. I smell the, what you call, eucalypt. The air is much more dry here."

We talked for a long time. I watched him smile and laugh. I watched him frown and look sad as he talked about his family and friends at home. His skin is smooth and caramel-colored.

He is so beautiful.

As the sun started to fade, Hiro stood up and stretched.

He walked back into the house to pack up his books. "I am playing cello tomorrow evening, at the park—six o'clock. Would you like to see?"

"I would love to!"

"Would Grace like to come?"

"I think she would."

He smiled, and said, "But not the cat."

I laughed. "No, I won't bring the cat."

As he sauntered off down the street I skipped around the lounge room, singing.

Say I love you, say I need you, say all the things that people say when love is new.

I skipped over to where Grace was sitting and planted a big kiss on her forehead.

"We have a date, Grace!"

I sat down at the dining table, where he had been sitting. I sat there thinking about his smile and his muscly calves.

I wondered what it would be like tomorrow. Busking with Hiro.

Later that night, when I had calmed down, I rang my mother.

"What happened to Anna?" I asked her.

"Who?"

"Anna. Remember? They used to live next door."

"Oh," said my mother. "Her parents were teachers. They got a transfer somewhere down south, I think."

"Can you remember where?" I asked.

"Oh, was it Kiama? Somewhere around there. Why the sudden interest?"

"I was just thinking, you know. Anna and I were good

friends and I just wondered what happened to her, that's all. I haven't had that many good friends and I thought I might look her up and see how she is."

"Good for you," said my mother.

I made myself a pint of coffee and sat down in Grace's study with the spooky box in front of me.

Grace was pregnant when she had the accident. Mr. Preston knew she was pregnant or he wouldn't have said "both of them" when he talked about how the accident was his fault. Mr. Preston said it was his fault.

I can hear Hiro's casual inquiry, *"Oh . . . what happened?"* echo in my head.

I never asked!

Why have I never asked? I've never asked because I thought it would be rude, like staring, like commenting on someone's weight gain—one just doesn't.

I remember standing in a line at a shop when I was about three or four years old. There was a woman in front of us. I observed her for a while, quietly hugging my mother's thigh, and then I looked up to my mother and said in a loud voice, "Look, Mummy, hasn't that lady got big boobs?" My mother went scarlet. The woman with the big boobs went scarlet.

"Shhh!" said my mother. I started to protest, "But she has, Mummy, look." I pointed with one chubby finger.

"Quiet now, darling, you don't talk about those sorts of things," said my mother.

"Why?"

"You just don't."

I lifted the lid from the spooky box and removed the ribbon-bound bundle.

Then I picked out the next sheet of paper and read.

No one can have their cake and eat it too.

We are not just having our cake, my love. We are sitting here in the candlelight, hiding here in the dark, digging our arms up to our elbows in luscious chocolate syrup and smearing jam and cream over our faces.

One day, one fine day, my delicious friend, someone is going to notice the crumbs on your chin. Someone is going to comment on the wildberry sauce on your shirtsleeve.

The difference we can make now is to choose, and to choose now to stop. Or, if not stop, then limit our appetite to the occasional brandy snap. Or if not stop, then . . .

Does the word "marriage" frighten you?

This is not just a wise choice but an essential one. Because those living on dry bread and tepid water will protest, loudly, if they find out what we are supping on here in the dark.

Go now, my delectable love, licking your fingers and wiping your mouth on the back of your wrist, and do not return, unless you plan to bring to me that shiny band of gold that would make our feasting so much less abhorrent to our associates.

Today is the day of my date with Hiro.

I thought I would make up a picnic for us to eat tonight.

There is a picnic basket on top of the kitchen cupboards. It has four plates and cutlery and plastic glasses strapped to the lid with little leather straps. It has a blue and green lining that unfolds into a little tablecloth.

I dress Grace and we walk down to the delicatessen. "Hello there, little chicken," says the Italian lady. "What can I do for you today?"

I buy some Tasmanian cheese, a big crusty loaf and some cold meats. I buy olives and roasted tomatoes.

I walk to the bottle shop and buy a bottle of white wine and a big bottle of water.

Grace and I walk home with our purchases. I sing loudly as we walk along the street.

"I thought that we would just be friends, things will never be the same again."

I can't seem to get that song out of my head.

At home, I pack my little picnic basket and take a blanket out of the linen cupboard.

I flick through Grace's wardrobe, looking for something to wear. I put on a long green dress and a little white cardigan. I pull my hair back into a ponytail.

I'm walking out the door and I suddenly have a thought. I run back and grab a bottle of insect repellent from under the sink.

Grace and I walk to the park carrying our picnic basket and blanket. As we turn the corner out of our street I can see a few other people with baskets and blankets.

Maybe there is something else on tonight? Oh well, at least we have the picnic basket.

As we approach the park I can see people flocking through the gates. The grass area is half-filled with blankets. Corks are popping left, right and center. There are fairy lights around the rotunda. It has been set up as a makeshift bar. The teahouse is packed.

I look around for Hiro. I'm never going to find him in this crowd.

Between the teahouse and the rotunda a scaffolding stage has been set up. There are speakers on either side. There are people in tuxedos wandering around the stage and roadies hitching up microphones.

"Rachel." I hear a voice behind me. Mr. Preston's brother, Anthony, is reclining on a blanket to my left.

"Oh, hello there."

"You look lovely tonight," he says, smiling that big gorgeous smile.

I've always been afraid of gorgeous people. They have that smugness about them. They make me feel gangly and silly.

"Come and sit with me for a while," says Anthony.

"Oh," I say.

Think of an excuse, quickly, before you fall over or do something stupid.

"I see my brother has got to you and told you what a roguish fellow I am," he said, grinning. "I don't bite, unless you want me to."

"Oh, um, no. He hasn't said anything. It's just that I'm supposed to be meeting someone else here."

"Fair enough," he said, looking out at the crowd.

"Rachel" booms over the loudspeaker; then there is a squeak as the microphone feeds back.

I look around, startled.

"Well, anyway, I'm not such a bad fellow," he said with that grin again. "Maybe sometime we could go out and you could find out for yourself?"

"Oh," I say, surprised. Is he asking me out? "Maybe."

"Rachel" comes out of the loudspeaker again. I look up at the stage. There is Hiro, standing in the middle of the stage, grinning and waving at me with both arms. He is wearing a tuxedo. His hair is pulled back in a ponytail. Roadies are crowded around him, plugging in leads and taping things down with electrical tape. When Hiro said he played the cello, I didn't know that he meant he was really *good*.

I wave back vigorously.

"I have to go," I say, turning back to Anthony.

He nods and smiles. "Another time then?"

I don't answer. Instead I smile back and walk away, dragging Grace behind me by the arm, weaving our way between the blankets to the stage.

"Hello!" says Hiro. He's got his hands on his hips and is looking down at me from the stage. "I saved a space," he says, pointing to a spot about ten meters away from the stage, where there is a pile of instrument cases. "I can sit here too, when we are not playing."

We move the instrument cases to one side and lay out the blanket. Hiro sits down and I help Grace onto the blanket.

"Are you nervous?" I ask.

Hiro shrugs. "This is not new to me. I enjoy making music with people. I play these when I was . . ." He holds his hand about a meter off the ground; then he laughs. ". . . Maybe not. Maybe more." He holds his hand higher, and laughs again. He leans back on his elbow.

"You look much . . ." He frowns. "No, what is it? Very beautiful." He raises an eyebrow at me.

Oh my God! Oh my God! Be cool, Rach. Be cool.

I blush. I turn around to open the picnic basket. "Thank you. Would you like something to eat?" I pull out the loaf of bread and put it in his hand.

He looks down at the loaf of bread suddenly in his hands. "Ah, no, thank you. I will eat after."

I snatch the bread back and thrust it into the basket.

That was not cool. Do something cool, quick.

I pull out the band that's holding my hair back and shake my hair out like they do on the shampoo ads.

That was fairly cool.

I run my hand through my hair. The buckle of my watch gets caught in my hair.

Ahh! Ahh!

He leans toward me and starts to pick at my hair. I can smell him. He smells sweet. I can see his Adam's apple under his caramel skin, right in front of my face.

"There," he says, smiling. His face is close to mine.

You could kiss him. Do it! Do it!

"Harold, we're up." A man in a dinner suit holding a violin is calling down from the stage.

Hiro stands up and brushes down his pants.

"Break a leg," I say.

"You tried that already," he says with a laugh. He bows slightly and walks away.

I watched as Hiro and the other three men settled into their places on the stage. They paused for a moment. The whole park went quiet. I felt a little delicious shiver of anticipation. Then they began.

It was beautiful. They had no sheet music, they just played, looking at each other. Hiro was frowning with concentration. A wisp of his hair came loose from the ponytail.

I looked at Grace. She was lying back on the grass with her eyes closed.

They played for about twenty minutes; then they stood up and bowed. The man with the violin picked up his microphone. "We'll just be taking a short break. Don't go away! We'll be back soon."

I could see Hiro at the side of the stage, drinking a bottle of water, while the man with the double bass was speaking to him. Hiro passed his cello to one of the roadies, poured some water in his hand and threw it over his head, smoothing down the loose hair.

I reached into the picnic basket and pulled out the bottle of wine. I eased the cork out and poured two glasses, handing one to Grace. I made two sandwiches of cheese and pastrami and roasted tomato and put one in Grace's other hand. I started to munch on my sandwich.

I looked up and saw Hiro waving at me from the side of the stage. I waved back, inhaled a piece of bread and started coughing uncontrollably. I coughed up the offending crumb and quickly looked up again, but Hiro was turned the other way talking to the violin man.

They sat down and started to play again.

I filled up our glasses again. I rather smugly rubbed some insect repellent on Grace's arms.

Who's a clever nerd, then?

At the end Hiro jumped off the stage and came and sat down on the blanket with his cello in its case at his feet. "I will eat your bread now," he said, smiling.

"That was wonderful."

He shrugged. "We played well today."

He reached into the picnic basket and pulled out a glass. I made him a sandwich and promptly dropped it on the blanket.

What is wrong *with you?*

I picked up the bits of sandwich and put them in one of the empty plastic bags.

"You are kind of, what do you say? Stupid?" He looked at my face. My jaw had dropped. "No, no, I think the word is clumsy?" Now he was embarrassed.

"Only when you are around," I said. "I am as agile as the next person, when you're not around."

"I make you, ahh . . . excited? Yes?"

Yes. Yes, you do.

I pulled out the insect repellent and handed it to him. "No, it's just . . . I don't know."

He was looking at the bottle, turning it over in his hands. "For the food?" he asks me.

"No," I laughed. "Here, you rub it on your arms." I demonstrated. While he rubbed the repellent on his arms I made him another sandwich, pulled out the wine and filled his glass.

We sat together, talking about music and watching the roadies pack up the gear, winding cords around their forearms.

We talked about television. "We have some of the same television at home. They do translating."

"Like 'Monkey Magic,' huh, Tripitaka," I said, "you know, Tripitaka?" I started singing, "Born from an egg on a mountaintop."

"No, I don't know, but you could sing some more," he said, leaning back on his elbows.

I'm imagining what he would look like with no shirt on.

Mmmmm, I bet he's got a muscly belly too.

After the roadies had packed all of the equipment, he sat up and looked at his watch. "We should be going home now?"

We packed up the picnic basket. He carried the blanket and his cello, and we walked toward the gate.

When we got to the gate he said to me, "Well, thank you for seeing." He pointed back toward the stage.

"My pleasure."

"I will see you again another day, maybe? Soon?" he

handed me the blanket, bowed at me again and walked away.

I watched him walking for a while. He had his hand in his pocket as he sauntered along. The dinner suit he was wearing exaggerated his square shoulders. He turned around, walking backward, and waved at me. I sighed.

"Well, Grace, he thinks I am a dill."

I took Grace by the arm and we walked home.

28

it's that *day again. It's that day when you sit down and try to rein in your rampant hangover and make some halfhearted but well-intentioned declarations about how exciting your life is going to be in the forthcoming year.*

Firstly, it's time to get your career in order. It's time to bite the bullet and leave Messrs. Preston and move into a company where you might even get a promotion one day. No more busting a gut. (Last year it was "no more busting egos" and look how long that lasted!)

You're not short of cash. Which reminds me, this year we're going to stop being angry about the project monstrosity that's been built on the rubble of the family home.

There's nothing much to keep you here, it's time to take "the big trip."

Resolution one: New York. This year you're going to New York.

Secondly, it's time to address the big M issue.

Gentle Chardonnay-inspired musings aside, it might be time to exert a little pressure.

* Note: is he "the one"?

M issue unresolved c/o to next New Year's Day.

New York it is. Time to bring back your b-b-bounce.

• • •

Grace is out with Jan. I am sitting in her study again. I have the spooky box in my lap. This is the last piece of paper.

It doesn't make any sense.

I throw the last note on the desk in disgust. I don't know what I thought she was going to tell me, but I thought it would be something new.

I untie the ribbon and flick through the papers again.

Give me a clue, Grace. What's it all about?

I don't know what I was hoping for. I do know that I thought there would be some hidden truth in it all. I thought this was the box of knowledge. I thought that when I got to the end of it I would understand what she was all about, what life was all about.

The only thing I have discovered is that Grace was a real person, before me, before the accident.

Grace had a life.

Before the accident.

Grace had a lover.

Before the accident.

Grace had thoughts and pain and anger and love and plans for the future.

Grace had a child.

All of a sudden, I am so sad for her. I am so sad.

She had people who loved her. She had a career. She had a baby.

I am suddenly overwhelmed with sorrow. There is no inner truth here. Here is just a person—just a life.

Grace wasn't a supermodel, she wasn't a genius, she was just an ordinary person living an ordinary life.

I sit at the desk and cry for Grace. How can this happen? What kind of life is this?

What kind of world is this?

What sort of person am I? What kind of person could live here with this person and never think about what has been lost? How selfish am I? I even had the nerve to be frightened of her. I am so ashamed of myself.

I am eighteen and I know a few things. One of the things that I thought I knew was that time will eventually heal all wounds. It hasn't healed Grace's wounds.

I am overwhelmed.

29

i'm so depressed. I'm inside a big, black, swollen rain cloud. The sadness is right through to my bones.

I want to go home. I miss my mum. I miss sitting on her veranda talking and laughing and not caring about anything. I miss Blueberry Day.

It's as if the truth, the real truth, that life is a bastard has hit me square in the belly and I'm reeling.

I am crying again. I want my mum. I'm tired. I'm depressed! I want to go home. I want to be a child again.

I ring my mum.

"Mum?"

"What is it, Rachel darling?"

"Mummy, I need you," I whisper softly. I can feel the prickle of tears in my eyes. I can feel the lump in my throat.

"I am sad," I say down the phone. I can feel the tenseness across my chest. I can't breathe.

"Mum?"

I'm listening hard now. The line is dead. I press the re-dial button but the phone rings out.

I hang up the phone and wander around the house whimpering to myself. I look at my red, blotchy face in the mirror and then curl up on the couch.

Twenty-eight minutes.

Twenty-eight minutes it took my mother to drive to my present location. I'm sitting on the couch, in my jammies and woolly socks, feeling sorry for myself.

I'm listening to Jeff Buckley. He makes me so sad. He's wailing at me passionately. I'm crying because I'm thinking Grace didn't get to say her last goodbye to whoever he was.

This is our last embrace, must I dream and always see your face?

Does she dream of her lover? The front door is open. The mynah birds are squawking at Prickles lying on the front step. I'm hugging my knees up to my chest and crying and singing with Jeff.

Kiss me, please, kiss me, but kiss me out of desire, babe, and not consolation.

I hear a car screech to a halt at the front of the house. I'm not listening. I am singing through my tears. I'm wallowing. Jeff is wailing, beautifully, passionately. I am sobbing.

I've got to listen to it all again.

I stand up and shuffle over to the CD player with my sad shoulders stooped. I put my sad hand out . . .

Collide, according to the pocket English dictionary, is to strike or dash together.

My mother came down the corridor so fast I didn't even see her. She was a blur. There was a sonic boom in the hallway as my mother hit the speed of sound. If the hallway had been any longer, she would have gone into warp speed.

"I'm here, my precious, I'm here. It's all right."

She nearly bowled me over.

I wrapped my arms around my mother's shoulders and cried and cried and cried.

Once my wailing had subsided a bit, my mother's first order of business was preparation of a nice cup of tea, followed closely by tucking of blankeys about my person.

"Now, what's all this then?"

"Grace had an accident," I said.

"Yes?" said my mother.

"But before that she had"—I waved my arms about—"she had beers! Don't you see? Beers on the veranda with the old blokes up the street, and they helped her with the gardening."

"Yes?"

"Well, she had a life." I blinked. "It wasn't very happy, but at least she had one!"

"I see," said my mother.

I drank my cup of tea. My mother put her hand over her mouth. Her shoulders hunched over. I thought she was going to be sick.

"Mum, what's wrong?"

She burst out laughing.

"What?"

"I'm sorry, sweetheart," she said, patting my leg. "How about I make you some nice hot soup? Or, I tell you what, we could have Tomato Night! What do you say? We'll have gazpacho and Bloody Marys and bruschetta and you can tell me what this is all about."

I frowned at my mother. "Why Tomato Night?"

"Well, with your head the way it is you won't need a costume," said my mother, and she burst out laughing again.

"Oh," I said. "Are you laughing at me?"

"Yes, of course, darling," said my mother.

I sat quietly drinking my tea while my mother bustled about in the kitchen making tomato-based little deliciouses.

"So tell me from the beginning," she said, settling on the lounge next to me. She picked up Prickles and placed him on her lap, smoothly stroking his fur. Prickles poked his little pink tongue out with bliss.

So I told how when I first moved in I hadn't paid much attention to Grace and when I did it was only from fear or disgust. I told her about Grace's sisters and how I didn't like them very much but I did think that they had problems. I told her about Mr. Preston and how he had loved her and still loved her and how sad that was for him. I told her about Herb and Bill and about Grace's parents. But I didn't tell her about the spooky box. I think I was ashamed.

My mother drank Bloody Marys, listened and patted the cat. At the end she nodded.

"Well?" I asked.

"Well, what?" asked my mother in return.

"Well, what's the answer?" I demanded.

"The answer to what?"

"Life!" I blustered.

"Forty-two," she replied, smiling. She put Prickles down.

"Very funny," I say. "But what's the real answer?"

"I don't know," she said with that indulgent smile.

"What do you mean?" I say. "You're old. I mean, older."

"Ask Nanna, she'll tell you," she said, laughing. "But seriously, that's what it's all about—the finding out. That's what makes it so much fun."

Mr. Preston came over to see Grace the next morning. My mother had gone out shopping. She bounced out the door in a bright blur of yellow. She has decided to stay with me for a couple of days.

"No doubt Brody will have some wild party while I am absent," she said as she left. "I daresay I shall have to overlook all manner of evidence when I return—not the least of which will be his dopey grin and extraordinary helpfulness."

I wandered about the house, tidying. I went out into the garden and picked some flowers.

Mr. Preston sat with Grace for a while and then she nodded off and he joined me on the veranda. We sat quietly. I bit my lip.

"What happened to Grace?"

"She banged her head."

"Yes, but how?"

"She banged it on the road."

I squinted out across the street. The sunshine was very bright. A nuisance of cats gamboled in the garden. Prickles was amongst them. They rolled about together, biting and kicking with both back feet. Then they lay indulgently in each other's arms. Mr. Preston frowned.

"Why won't you tell me?"

"Do you have a brother, chum?" he asked me.

"Yes, Brody. It means unusual beard, you know. He's a bit of a dill, but we get on all right."

Mr. Preston frowned. "Unusual beard."

"Yes," I said, blushing, "my mother is whimsical."

Mr. Preston sighed. Then he began.

"You know I have a brother. He worked in our office, as did my father and as did our father's father before him." Mr. Preston was drinking tea, Earl Grey, hot. I hate it but tolerate it, because it's what Jean-Luc Picard drinks when he is upset.

"Anthony was always destined for bigger things. He had empires to build, egos to crush." Mr. Preston was slurping on his tea. He had one ankle on his knee.

"I was beginning to build a relationship with Grace. I think she had finally decided to stop battling with me and we were becoming friends—good friends—but that was all. I was still married.

"I spent time with Grace, we worked closely together, but our relationship was a professional friendship and that was all, as far as Grace was concerned. That was all that I could offer. So I spent my days being stoically tragic about the whole thing."

Mr. Preston was quiet. He was perfectly still. I blinked in the sunshine. A gentle breeze played in my hair, blowing it across my face.

"That's how I used to be, you see? Mr. Roll-with-the-punches. I had my share of free lunches. I did favors where I shouldn't and took them in my turn. I greased the wheels on occasion."

Mr. Preston turned his cup around and around in his hand.

"Now I'm Mr. Patron. I volunteer for any number of community causes—environment groups, progress associations—busy, busy. Now I stand about being stoically tragic on behalf of others and sometimes I even make a difference, which is nice. Sometimes it makes me feel a bit better about my decades of selfishness."

Mr. Preston paused for a moment and took a deep breath.

My mother's car came careering down the street and pulled up with a jolt in front of the house, behind Mr. Preston's car.

Mr. Preston frowned as he watched her bounce out of the car.

"Hello, Rachel darling," she said as she threw the back door open and started to gather her bags of shopping.

Mr. Preston quickly strode down the steps and out the gate and took the bags from her.

"Why, thank you!" said my mother, beaming.

"My pleasure," said Mr. Preston, beaming back.

"Mr. Preston, this is my mother," I say.

"Miriam," said my mother.

"I'm Alistair Preston. Pleased to meet you."

"Alistair," said my mother.

"Miriam," said Mr. Preston, and then they both laughed.

Mr. Preston carried my mother's shopping into the kitchen and helped her unpack.

"My little chum tells me you are whimsical," observed Mr. Preston.

"Does she?" she asked, winking at me.

I sat on the couch and cringed.

Mr. Preston left. I followed him out to the front veranda.

"You were telling me something," I prompted.

"About what?"

"About your brother."

"Oh," he said. He leaned against the railing with his hip and folded his arms.

"When we were boys," he began, "I was given a spaniel bitch for my birthday. Anthony, my brother—he could see how much I loved the dog, and set out to steal her from me. For months Anthony trained the dog to come to his call. One day the dog was in the road. I was on one side of the road and Anthony was on the other. There was a car coming along the road, so I called the dog. I just wanted her to be safe. Anthony called the dog from the other side."

Mr. Preston pulled his hair back from his forehead. He crossed one foot over the other and looked out into the street.

"There was a battle going on. I was looking at Anthony and he was looking at me and the car was approaching. Anthony called the dog again and she went to him."

Mr. Preston paused for a long while.

"He had won. After that he ignored the dog completely. It was about winning. It was about beating me. We gave the dog away. I couldn't look at her without feeling the betrayal." Mr. Preston laughed bitterly. "A dog—a bloody dog. I had to attach all these emotional ties to it."

He shook his head. "Ridiculous."

He stepped lightly down the steps and out the gate.

"See you," I said.

He nodded as he opened his car door, climbed in and drove away.

"You didn't tell me he was handsome!" said my mother when he had gone. She fluffed her yellow blouse. "Heavens!" she said. "I think I even felt a little stirring!"

"Mum! Please!"

"Well, I did," she protested.

Having tired of my continual complaints and obvious distress about having to cook meals, my mother had thoughtfully purchased two cookbooks for me during her shopping trip.

I studied them on the lounge whilst my mother prepared something luscious and far beyond my present level of competence.

The first cookbook, *Banquet in Brief*, was dedicated to meals that could be prepared in a very short time. It seemed to comprise, almost exclusively, recipes for things on toast; for example, cheese on toast. It then substantially increased in complexity to such elaborate dishes as ham, tomato and cheese on toast. I threw *Banquet in Brief* on the coffee table in disgust and picked up the next.

The second cookbook, *Epiconomy*, was dedicated to

low-budget meals and included a great many recipes using mince as the main ingredient. Savory mince seemed to be the hero of the book and wore many guises. It was always distinguishable to the reader, though, because of its consistent savoriness and strong mince undertones.

"Thanks for that, Mum," I called across the room.

"My pleasure, Rachel darling," she replied from within a cloud of saffron-scented steam.

"I was thinking," she said, "you could go to the post office."

"What?"

"Don't say what, say I beg your pardon."

"I beg your pardon?"

"To look up your friend Anna. Remember? You asked me where she had moved to. They would have telephone directories there and you could look her up."

I lay on the couch with my arms behind my head and jiggled my feet.

"Amanda is getting married."

"Oh, really?" said my mother, clattering about in Grace's cupboards.

"To Bozza. Can you believe it?" I said.

"Well, Rachel darling, maybe he makes her happy," said my mother.

I hrumphed and jiggled my feet some more.

"How do you know that he doesn't?" she asked, pausing for a moment to look at me.

"He's titillated by the discoloration of ceramic tiles, Mother! He's not her intellectual equal!"

She put down the saucepan she was holding and leaned against the kitchen bench. "There is this tradition, I don't know whether you've heard of it," she began, "where a young woman seeks an amiable fellow who will be able to provide for her and her children, should she choose to have them. Then she dresses in a magnificent frock and promises to be with him forever. It's called marriage, and whilst you have not experienced marriage yourself or by direct observation through me, an awful lot of people do it. I imagine, for some, it would be an enormous comfort to have a piece of paper guaranteeing eternal love."

I frowned at her and jiggled some more.

"I think you are fabulous, darling, I think you are beautiful and clever, but I must say, you have a propensity to judge everybody by your own standards. It is a bad habit to get into, my love, because you will never be satisfied with anyone."

"That's not true," I said, folding my arms across my chest.

"Oh yes it is, my sweet," said my mother, pointing at me with a slotted spoon.

"I'm very tolerant!"

"Only of people who do exactly as you would have them do."

Not being able to think of a clever rebuttal, I stomped about on the timber floor in my socked feet. My mother watched me from the corner of her eye and hummed cheerfully to herself.

After half an hour of bad-tempered stomping my mother asked, "Why don't you ask that handsome Alistair over for dinner?"

"Why didn't you ask him yourself?" I replied. I was still a little raw about the "intolerant" remark.

"Well," she said, "Thai dishes can be so volatile. I wanted to be sure of its scrumptiousness before imposing it upon anyone else."

"Why don't you ring him?" I said.

"All right then, I will," she replied.

She shook her hands in the air above her head, allowing gravity to pull the sleeves of her shirt back to her elbows, and picked up my address book next to the phone.

I am eighteen and have recently discovered that I know very little (and am bound to find that I know even less if my mother stays for much longer), but my mother is a living example of the expression "no hide, no Christmas box." She never hesitates. She shows no fear or reticence. One of the many reasons that I admire her is for her intrepidness.

Mr. Preston was otherwise engaged but agreed to join us on the following night.

"Never mind," said my mother, serving the Thai (which proved to be as scrumptious as she had anticipated), "I shall just have to cook something as mind-blowingly stunning tomorrow."

32

Of all days, today I dragged out my old, scuffed, dirty Ugg boots. Of all days, today I found my striped beanie with the pompom on top. Today, of all days, Hiro decided to drop around. I stood in the doorway in my beanie and my Ugg boots and quietly dissolved into pure embarrassment.

Hiro smiled with amusement. He followed me as I flip-flopped into the lounge room. I couldn't exactly take them off now, could I? The damage had been done. Besides, I knew that underneath I had beanie hair, which was probably worse, on the whole.

I tried to think of something scintillating to say, to show that my intellect was beyond fashion. It didn't work.

My mother was sitting out back with Grace, chattering and laughing.

"I thought maybe we could, you know, walk?" he said to me.

"Walk where?"

"Well, maybe to the music shop? I would like to show you some special songs."

"OK, I'll just have to check with my mother."

Check with my mother? How embarrassing. Things are getting worse.

I flip-flopped out the back. "Mum, this is Hiro."

My mother's eyes flicked toward my beanie and then my Ugg boots, and she grinned.

"Come and sit out here with me, Hiro. Then Rachel can go and discreetly get out of that ridiculous hat," she purred, patting the seat beside her.

"Umm, actually, my name is Harold," said Hiro.

My mother's eyes widened just that little bit and then she said, "Well, a rose by any other name and all that. Come and tell me about yourself."

I almost-ran back to my room and tried to repair my head. It was no use. I piled my hair up in a big heap on my head and fastened it with a clip. I pulled on some jeans and a jumper. I dabbed some powder on my nose and quickly applied some mascara to my lashes. Then I threw my Ugg boots across the room in disgust and pulled on some sneakers.

I could hear my mother as I walked back through the house.

"Cello, really? How intriguing. My youngest plays the euphonium, you know. Such a bold and powerful instrument, the euphonium—beefs up the brass section no end, don't you think?"

She turned toward me as I walked down the step.

"Ah, there we are. No fez, darling? No cheery bonnet, I see?" she said, winking at me.

Hiro laughed.

"Oh yes! Let's all poke fun at Rachel. Highly amusing, yes," I said, smiling back just as cheerfully. "You'll keep."

"Well, you go off and have fun then. Grace and I will hold the fort," my mother said.

Hiro and I walked down to the main street, our hands brushing together occasionally. I liked it.

"Music is very important to me," he said as we walked. "I think it . . . What is the word? Endurance? When there is nothing there is always music, do you know what I mean?"

I nodded. I liked music too. I wasn't sure what he was trying to say, but he was close to me and that was a buzz.

In the music shop, Hiro took me over to the machine with the headphones, then wandered around picking CDs for me to listen to.

"Here, this is Albinoni. Very sad and very beautiful. This sounds to me like a thousand broken hearts. You must listen to it loudly and let your heart break too."

I closed my eyes and listened.

"Do you like that one?" he asked me, smiling.

"It's so sad!" I said, finding myself choked up.

"Isn't it? Strings are very good at breaking the heart."

He reached forward and replaced that CD with another. "Here, this is Pachelbel. You will know this one already, maybe. I like this one because of its, umm . . . layers of sounds. This one lifts the spirit. It makes you feel strong."

Hiro brought me more music. Before each piece he would tell me how it made him feel and what he liked about it. After each explanation I would close my eyes and listen.

On the way back, we stopped at the post office. I wrote down a list of all the phone numbers that might be Anna's.

Hiro walked back with me to my front door. He stood on the veranda with his hands in his pockets.

"Thank you so much," I said. "That was lovely. It was a really nice gift. I don't know anything about classical music."

He grinned. "I would like to show you more. There is so much to know," he said. "Maybe I will play for you, also?"

"That would be great."

Then he leaned forward and kissed me. He put his hand flat on the small of my back. His lips were warm. I may have even let a soft moan escape.

33

At university, after my lecture, I stop by the cafeteria to see if there is anyone I know. Kate is perched in her favorite corner.

I sit with Kate and the pert girl with the funky glasses whose name has turned out to be Suzette (which I had always thought was a crepey type of dessert, but apparently not).

"So, have you realized your destiny yet?" asks Suzette as I sit down.

"Not yet," I say. I throw my notes on the seat next to me.

"What's it to be, then?" asks Kate. "A brutally white lab coat or a caftan and lashings of chamomile tea?"

"What's all this?" asks Suzette.

I explain to her about Grace, and about how Kate thought that working with people was out of character for me.

"Really?" she asks, sitting back. "That sounds like an interesting job."

"So what's this destiny you're after?" asks Kate with a gleam in her eye.

"Well," I say, eyeing them closely for ridicule, "can I tell you what I really want to do?"

"Of course!" replies Suzette, leaning forward.

"I think I want to solve mysteries," I say, smiling.

"Like a detective?" says Suzette.

"You could be one of those forensic psychologists—like in all those murder novels!" says Kate.

"You'd probably have to do heaps of degrees," says Suzette, "and you'd have to be full of angst and never be able to sustain a fulfilling relationship."

"But they always seem to be wearing funky suits under their trench coats, don't they?"

"Yes, and they always tend to be the only woman toughing it out in a man's world."

"And they spend an awful lot of time thinking about dead people," continues Kate. "It'd be rough trying to stay upbeat when you think about dead people all day and all night."

"That's what I said," says Suzette. "That'd be where all your angst comes in."

"You could do angst," says Kate brightly, patting me on the arm.

"Yes, but can you *maintain* angst?" asks Suzette.

"Sure, she can. She can do grim. I've seen grim."

"Yes, but grim is different from angst, isn't it?" says Suzette. "Grim is more your, sort of, angst without philosophical dilemma."

"Yes, but they're siblings in the range of dispositions—angst and grimness, don't you think?" asks Kate.

"No, angst is far more intellectual than grim. I would have said that grim is more like angst's half-witted second cousin."

"When have you seen me do grim?" I ask.

"All the time in the café. You used to do a great grim when there was less cream of mushroom soup than cream of mushroom soup orderers," replied Kate.

"That wasn't grim, that was concentration."

"Well," said Suzette, encouraged by this latest piece of information, "if your concentration looks like grim—that's a start, isn't it?"

"You'll still need a funky suit and a trench coat," adds Kate.

I look at my watch and decide it is time to go home.

I walk into the house and am almost overcome by the volume of Edith Piaf. My mother is out back, walking up the pathway with Herb and Bill. Grace stands by her with her hands behind her back. She turns as I approach, and for a moment I think I see recognition flash across her face.

"Grace!" I say. "Hello there, turtledove."

I walk up to her and pat her on the shoulder.

"Oh, hello, Rachel darling," says my mother. "It seems these fellows know everything there is to know about camellias and gardenias and almost everything else pretty and pungent. So what do you think of that, then?"

"Grace knows who I am," I say.

"Well, of course she does," says my mother, "you've lived here for what? Ever so long. Anyway, William, what can you tell me about hydrangeas? I know some sort of soil is supposed to make them pink and some other makes them blue, but for the life of me I can never remember which."

I leave the four of them to wander about the garden some more and walk back inside to get myself a cool drink.

I decide to ring all the numbers that might be Anna's. The first two are wrong numbers but the third is an answering machine. It might have been Anna's mother, but I can't say for sure. I feel really nervous but I leave a message anyway.

"Hello, this is Rachel. I used to live in Clements Street. I don't know if you remember me, or even if this is the right number. I'm looking for Anna who used to live next door. I was thinking about old friends. I just wondered how you were doing. Anyway, this is my number if you want to call me."

I'm just hanging up the phone when I hear a tentative knock. Mr. Preston is standing in the doorway.

"Hello there, chum," I say. "Come in, then. Can I get you something to drink?"

Mr. Preston accepts and joins me in the kitchen.

"I saw your brother the other day in the park," I say, pouring some cold water into a glass. "He asked me out, the cheeky devil."

"He did what?" says Mr. Preston. He reaches forward and takes hold of me by the arm. "And you refused, didn't you?" he says, glaring at me.

I look down at his hand on my arm. He lets go.

"I'm sorry," he says.

He paces the kitchen for a moment.

"I don't want you to go," he says. "He's much older than you, to start with. And he's not a nice bloke!"

"Yes," I answer. "He thought that you would say that."

Mr. Preston snorts. "That would be right."

"What is this issue you have?" I ask.

"I do not have an issue!" he yells at me.

"Obviously."

Mr. Preston sits down on the lounge.

"I told you a little bit about him the other day," he says. He seems to have calmed down a little bit.

I sit next to him and wait.

"He's not good with women," he says. "Actually, he's very good with women, and that's the problem."

I take a sip of my water.

"Don't you see?" he asks me. "He must think I have some sort of design on you. I don't, by the way. But if he thinks it, he will try very hard."

"I don't understand."

Mr. Preston rubs his chin in an agitated way. He begins, "A long time ago—before . . . Anthony could see my interest in Grace, and as he had done so many times before, he set out to steal her from me. He never had any trouble attracting women, but this woman was a challenge for him, because he knew that I wanted her. He knew that I cared for her."

He put both hands over his face and sighed.

"It started with small victories. He would ask her to lunch when he knew we had arranged to eat together. He would grin at me as he swanned out of the office with Grace on his arm. He would bring her extravagant gifts. I didn't buy her anything—except once I bought her a gold bracelet. Then I was ashamed of myself for getting involved in his war. I became . . . angry. I couldn't have her. I had tried not to care for Grace. I tried . . ."

Mr. Preston went on. "More than anything, I didn't want Grace to become like the spaniel bitch that I couldn't look at, that I kicked away, that I despised. I couldn't have Grace, but I didn't want Anthony to have her either. He didn't care for her, he didn't love her, he just wanted to 'win.' She was just a new spaniel bitch."

I sat still, waiting for him to go on.

"You see?" he said, fixing me in his gaze. "It's just like Grace all over again. He doesn't *like* you, he just . . ."

I looked down at my glass. I spoke very slowly and very deliberately. "I didn't accept his offer. He's not my type. I think you are reading too much into this. I think you have all this anger with your brother and it's affecting your life."

Mr. Preston nodded. Then laughed.

"How old are you, seventeen? Eighteen?" he said.

"Eighteen," I replied.

"You know too much for an eighteen-year-old," he said. Then he pinched me on the cheek.

"Alistair," said my mother, swanning in the back door. She had a bunch of rosemary in her hand and was fanning her face with it.

"Miriam," replied Mr. Preston, and then they both laughed.

Normally my mother cooks, but not tonight. Tonight she sat on the couch with Grace and Mr. Preston and barked orders.

"Put some new potatoes in some hot water and put them on the stove on a medium-to-high heat," she said to me. Then she turned to Mr. Preston without a pause. "Oh yes, I agree. Venice is lovely in the spring, isn't it?"

"Cut those carrots long-wise, darling," she said a couple

of minutes later, and then turned back to Mr. Preston. "Of course, *everyone* gets sick in India, but I have a cast-iron constitution. My youngest is allergic to lychees, you know. Do you have children?"

Then she turned back to me. "We need some more wine out here, darling," she said, then turned back to Mr. Preston. "What a shame for you. Terribly useful, children. A bit trying for the first couple of years, but terribly useful after that."

I opened a new bottle of wine and brought it over to the coffee table.

"Just slosh that meat in the marinade, Rachel. No, slosh it—slosh, slosh. Like gold panning. You know how to pan for gold, don't you?" she said to me over her shoulder, and then turned back to Mr. Preston. "So, what happened then?"

"I left my wife. Or, she left me. We left each other, in any case," said Mr. Preston, refilling his wineglass. He sat back and sighed again.

"Oh, what a shame. She sounded lovely," said my mother. Then she called out over her shoulder. "Just a splosh of olive oil on those potatoes, my sweet one."

I sploshed the potatoes as directed.

"So things worked out with Grace, then?" my mother asked Mr. Preston. My ears pricked up.

"Ahh, no," he said, wistfully. He looked up at me and gave me a wink. "So tell me about young Rachel here," he said, smiling.

"She is my *favorite* daughter," said my mother, reaching over and patting Mr. Preston on the leg.

"I'm your only daughter," I call out from the kitchen.

"Yes, and you're my favorite one."

She rose regally from the lounge to serve the meal.

As she placed it on the table, she said, "There now, does that not look divine? I hope you enjoy this, Alistair. It's one of my best."

"I did all the cooking," I protested.

Mother put her hand over her heart and fluttered her eyelids dramatically. "How sharper than a serpent's tooth it is to have a thankless child," she quoted.

While we ate, my mother continued to show off shamelessly. She spoke animatedly and Mr. Preston and I watched with appreciation.

After the meal they sat together on the lounge while I prepared Grace for bed. I could hear their laughter from where we stood in Grace's bedroom.

I sat next to her on the bed for a little while.

"Good night, Gracey," I said.

She looked through my face for a moment and I leaned forward to smooth down her hair.

"You knew who I was today," I said to her. "That's something, isn't it?"

I kissed her on the forehead and turned out the bedside lamp.

I walked into the kitchen to make coffee for my mother and Mr. Preston.

My mother sat on the couch with one knee hugged against her chest. They were talking quietly together.

"Yes, my children do give me a great deal of pleasure," she was saying, softly. "The first time I saw Rachel's face, that changed my life forever. Children do that. I looked down at her and thought, hey, there's a little wee part of me. I'm quite ferocious about her—about them both."

I put the coffee on the table before them and settled in on the corner of the lounge next to my mother.

"Did you ever think of having children?" my mother asked Mr. Preston.

He sat still for a moment and frowned. "My wife would bring it up on occasion and we would talk about it. I would say that I wanted to be there more often and be able to take time to spend with the child and that I couldn't do that while I was working this way and could we put it off just one more year while I got things settled at work."

My mother leaned forward and poured the coffee.

"All that was true," Mr. Preston continued, "but I was also selfish and wanted her to myself and knew that any child would take her attention away from me."

My mother handed him a cup of coffee. "Yes, men are greedy and completely egotistical for the most part, but at least you are able to admit it."

Mr. Preston smiled and took the coffee from her.

"So what about children and Grace?" asked my mother.

Mr. Preston turned to me. "How do you know about that?"

"She didn't," I replied, pointing to my mother. "Grace's sister told me, though."

"She's the cat's mother," said Mr. Preston, and took a slurp of his coffee. "One day Grace phoned me and asked me to come to the house. She had . . . fallen pregnant to Anthony. That's my brother. She wanted to ask me what to do. I was such a *dear friend*, you see? Should she tell him about the child? How would he respond? Would he look after her? We sat here in this room."

Mr. Preston sniffed. He brought a handkerchief out of his pocket and wiped his nose. "Oh dear."

My mother leaned forward and refilled his cup.

"I, of course, knew that Anthony would not be interested in Grace anymore. The cost to Grace was irrelevant. The cost to me . . . well."

Mr. Preston picked up his cup and drank noisily.

"I felt I had to tell her the truth," he said. "I should have thought about it for a while but I didn't because I was cranky."

My mother leaned toward me and put her hand on my knee.

"That must have been pretty rough," she said.

Mr. Preston blew his nose. "Yep," he said, "it was pretty rough. Anyway, what can you do? It's all over now."

"What happened after that?" I asked.

"Oh, she got angry with me, she said I was jealous. She said I was too weak. She said I was trying to hurt her. We shouted at each other for a little while."

Mr. Preston closed his eyes and ran his thumb and index finger across his eyebrows.

"That was the last thing we said to each other before the accident. I was angry, she was angry. We both said mean things. I have a really shocking temper."

My mother nodded. "Classic Type A personality."

He looked up at me and said, "Can I have a Scotch or something? This is all a bit much."

I stood up and walked into the kitchen and made us all a drink, bringing the bottle back to the table with me.

"Anyway, I knew that Anthony was taking another girl

out that night, you see? I also knew that he took them all to the same place. I dragged her out to my car. She was still yelling at me. We got into the car. For a little while she tried to argue with me. She called me names, but as she watched where we were going, as we approached the waterfront, she became very quiet."

Mr. Preston downed his drink and held it out to me for another.

"There used to be a little restaurant on the waterfront. It doesn't exist anymore since that whole area has been re-developed. My father would take us there every so often, Anthony and me. He was very friendly with the owners—a Chinese family. It was very simple. It was really just at the back of a house, between warehouses. They didn't have a license and eventually the council closed it down. My father and I, we had some mates on the council. We held them off as long as we could—encouraged them to turn a blind eye."

He looked at me. "I used to grease the wheels on occasion, you see?"

He poured himself another drink. "They didn't speak English, so you pretty much ate what they gave you. There were about thirteen tiny courses, all authentic. There were only about five tables. There were no fancy tablecloths, no fancy cutlery. It was just good food, good wine, a great view out over the water."

Mr. Preston swirled the last of his Scotch around in his glass.

"It used to be a special place for my father and Anthony and me—just the boys. But after my father died, Anthony started to take his girls there. That really pissed me off. Excuse me."

Mr. Preston took his handkerchief out of his pocket and blew his nose again.

"I pulled up at the curb a little way from the restaurant and we walked. The road is very narrow and there are a lot of trucks coming to and from the docks. The ships are unloading there twenty-four hours. Grace was moving very slowly. Her face was white and pinched. She knew what she was going to see. I knew she didn't want to see."

Mr. Preston took a deep breath.

"We came to the restaurant along a narrow dark street. Grace was moving slowly, like a sleepwalker. We went past the warehouse and rounded the corner. Anthony was there, sitting at the farthest table closest to the water with a very pretty, very young girl. He likes them young.

"I looked at Grace. Tears were rolling down her cheeks. Flooding down. They were sliding down her neck. Her mascara was running. I remember thinking that I'd never seen her makeup run.

"Anthony looked up and saw us standing there. He saw Grace standing there on the path outside his special restaurant. Beautiful, elegant Grace, with tears rolling down her face."

Mr. Preston was crying. He rubbed his face with the back of his hand.

"I'm sorry," he said, "you know I think about this all the time. I don't normally cry."

"That's all right," said my mother, leaning over the table toward him. "It's very refreshing, actually. Please go on."

Mr. Preston took another deep breath and refilled his glass.

"Well, then Anthony turned back to the girl he was with

and placed his hand over hers on the table," Mr. Preston said, placing one of his own hands across the other.

"Grace gave out a small whimpering, whining noise. It was an animal noise. It was the sound of . . . of *pain*. She doubled over, clutching her stomach as if she had been hit."

Mr. Preston wiped his nose again with his handkerchief. Tears were coursing down his cheeks. He talked with his eyes closed.

"This is the moment that I will remember for the rest of my life. Every day, this scene occurs over and over in my mind. I wake up to this image every morning of every day of my life.

"Grace staggered backward. Grace stepped back into the middle of the road. I can hear the blast of the horn. I can see the headlights on Grace like some . . . like some ghastly spotlight. Grace's head turning to see the truck bearing down. Her face lit up in the darkness. Now I can hear brakes screaming and the screaming from my own mouth.

"The truck couldn't have been moving very fast. It was a narrow street with lots of corners. Big trucks are coming through there all the time, loading up from the ships. They all move faster than they should. A fully loaded truck takes such a bloody long time to stop, you see?"

Mr. Preston still had his eyes closed. The tears were falling down his cheeks and splashing onto his shirt.

"Grace tries to move forward but twists on her ankle and she's falling down, like slow motion. She puts her arms up in front of her. For an instant her face is in shadow out of the truck's headlights. She's falling, falling even before the truck hits her."

He opens his eyes again and takes a swig of his drink.

"I feel pain. I feel strong pain and realize that I have dropped to my knees on the path. I feel the breath rush out of my lungs. For a moment I'm on my knees on the path with no air in my lungs. I'm watching the truck pulling up. I'm thinking she's going to make it!

"The truck is almost stopped when it hits her. I don't know, maybe if she hadn't been off balance already . . .

"The truck hits her and she hits the road. She just kind of crumples. Her head strikes the road just above the temple."

Mr. Preston taps his middle finger on the temple just above his left eyebrow.

"I scrabble over to where she is lying. I don't bother trying to get to my feet. I get there on my hands and knees. I can hear a noise coming from my throat, I can't breathe. I lift her head and hold her to me. Her eyes are closed. There is a graze on her cheek. She looks all right to me. Thank Christ, I'm thinking to myself. Then I shift and I can see her properly in the headlights of the truck. Her eyes are blank—they're just blank. There is blood coming out of her ears—a lot of it."

Mr. Preston looks up at us. He wipes his face with his handkerchief.

My mother is sitting on the couch next to me with tears sliding down her cheeks.

My mother went home this morning. I miss her already. Now it's just Grace and me again. I think she liked the hullabaloo of people around her.

Grace and I sat on the front veranda in the sunshine.

Hiro arrived at about ten. He brought Grace and me a croissant and we had a little picnic on the front steps. I managed to get through the whole meal without spilling anything or falling over, so I'm fairly proud of myself. He asked me to a film festival they're holding at uni next week.

"There are some animations," he said. "Do you like animations?"

"Yes," I said, smiling.

After breakfast, Kate, Suzette and the dreadlock boy turned up. We sat on the front veranda talking and drinking coffee. The dreadlock boy had some reggae CDs in his bag and we listened to them for a while. Hiro and the dreadlock boy sat together on the grass and talked about music.

"I think music is more pervasive and powerful than religion," the dreadlock boy said.

"Oh, you talk a lot of crap," interrupted Suzette.

"No, you don't understand," said the dreadlock boy, turning to her, "every culture has music. It plots the course of our evolution. Music represents the ideology of the people and the times."

"OK, you nong. What about 'She Bangs'?" asked Suzette.

"Well, that's a perfect example of a completely hedonistic society obsessed by the female form, incessantly using sexuality to sell superfluous products to increasingly excessive and television-anesthetized consumers."

I walked inside to boil the jug again and when I came back out, Herb and Bill were leaning over the fence talking to Kate.

"Morning, Miss Rachel," said Herb, waving to me.

"Morning, Herb," I replied.

Standing in the doorway, I looked around and saw people relaxing in my front garden. I realized that I have started to make friends. All these people have come here to spend time with me. They feel comfortable with me. They even like me.

Suzette was sitting on the arm of Grace's chair. While

she was talking she leaned down and absently stroked a strand of Grace's hair out of her eyes. The gesture was somehow carefree and affectionate at the same time. It made me smile.

"Do you know what you want to do now?" Kate asked me when I sat down.

"I think I want to work with people," I said. "People with acquired brain injuries like Grace."

Kate nodded. "You'll be good at that," she said.

In the early afternoon they left, two by two. Kate and Suzette were going to the library. Hiro and the dreadlock boy decided to go skateboarding. Herb and Bill continued their meander down the street.

When Hiro left, he kissed me on the cheek and then he blushed. Things may turn out yet.

The light was blinking on the answering machine. I pressed the Message button and listened.

"Rachel, this is Anna. Mum gave me your number. I was really surprised to hear from you. You know, you sort of lose touch with people. I'm living in Sydney now. It would be great to catch up with you, though. Give me a call."

I wrote her name and number down in the address book next to the phone. I flicked through the pages and found the number for Yvonne. I punched in the number and listened to the dial tone.

"Hello?"

"Hello, Yvonne?" I asked.

"Yes," the voice replied.

"This is Rachel. I am Grace's carer?"

"Oh, yes," she said.

"I just wanted you to know that Grace was thinking of you. She wrote a letter before the accident. I don't know if you ever received it."

"No, I haven't heard from Grace in a long time."

"Well, if you wanted, you could come and see her," I said. "I think she would like to see you. The letter . . . it was really nice. The letter says that she was very fond of you. I think it's important that you know that."

"Thank you," said Yvonne. "I would like to see her. The last time we spoke, we . . . we didn't part on good terms."

"Well, you can just come around whenever. You know, if you are in the area, or whatever."

"Thank you, Rachel."

As I hung up the phone I felt much better. The spooky box was so full of ghosts, bad thoughts, frustration and ill feeling. It was so full of things left unsaid. I might not be able to heal all of Grace's wounds, but at least with Yvonne I had healed one.

It was quiet again. Quiet and empty. But if it hadn't been so quiet, I might have missed something—something special.

I'm eighteen and I know a great many things but I don't know everything (for example, "A stitch in time saves Nine," what does that mean? My whole life, I've never known what that means. With what sort of needle does one stitch time? Who's Nine?). But I am learning.

Grace was in her chair by the window. I moved her chair so it faced the back garden. I thought she could watch the birds that have moved into the mulberry tree. They have chicks, and the parent birds are always flying in and out getting little grubs for them. Grace was in her chair looking out the window.

I wasn't playing any music. I usually play music in the afternoon, jazz, or blues, but not today. I could hear the birds chirruping and squabbling in the mulberry tree. I could hear the occasional car as it passed in the street, trains in the distance. I could hear all the sounds of suburbia on a sunny afternoon. Then, very faintly, I could hear another sound. I stood very still and listened. I had my eyes closed, my hand cupped behind my ear.

I could hear Grace.

I moved very quietly toward her, tiptoeing across the wooden floor. I knelt down behind her chair on the floor. Nothing. No sound but the birds and the cars. I shut my eyes and listened.

There it was again!

She was sitting perfectly still. I knelt down behind her. I could hear something.

Grace was singing.

Ever so gently, ever so softly. No words, just a tune, breathy. "La, la, da, da."

I sat there on the floor behind Grace's chair listening. Listening to Grace sing. Sat there, on the hard wooden floor, with my eyes squeezed shut, listening to Grace sing.

Never before had I heard a single sound from Grace that was voluntary. Never before had I heard her voice.

I sat there on the floor behind Grace's chair, a tear rolling down my cheek, and listened as Grace sang.

When I opened my eyes, I could see her finger ever so slightly tapping the arm of the chair, tapping to the beat, "La, la, da, da." Tap, tap, tap.

I don't know how long I sat there, but I heard her. I heard Grace.

When there is nothing, there is always music. I know what that means now.

She's in there. I know she is.

about the author

Alyssa Brugman was born in an elderly people's home in the Australian city of Lake Macquarie (it was the closest medical facility). She attended five different schools before completing a business degree at Newcastle University. She now lives in Sydney and is a full-time writer. Her previous novel, *Walking Naked*, was published by Delacorte Press.